W9-AWD-442

"Ma'am, can you hear me?" Whit studied the woman, who clung to the child. Harry's child. Whit's half niece.

A child Whit hadn't met because of the complications of family.

"Ma'am—"

She gasped. "Don't touch her."

Although he heard a siren wailing in the distance, he knew it would take a few minutes before they arrived on the scene.

A lot could happen in a few minutes.

It sounded like the perps had already done some major damage, breaking into the house and potentially shooting his half brother and wife.

Whit had to shelve his panic over losing his brother and focus on protecting the baby and the woman clinging to her.

The baby squeaked. She was his blood, his family, and Whit wouldn't let anything happen to her.

Apparently, the nanny felt the same way.

"Ma'am, my name is Brody Whittaker. I'm in town to visit Harry and I heard the gunshots. I'd like to help."

That got her to open her eyes.

An eternal optimist, **Hope White** was born and raised in the Midwest. She and her college sweetheart have been married for thirty years and are blessed with two wonderful sons, two feisty cats and a bossy border collie. When not dreaming up inspirational tales, Hope enjoys hiking, sipping tea with friends and going to the movies. She loves to hear from readers, who can contact her at hopewhiteauthor@gmail.com.

Books by Hope White

Love Inspired Suspense

Hidden in Shadows
Witness on the Run
Christmas Haven
Small Town Protector
Safe Harbor
Baby on the Run
Nanny Witness

Echo Mountain

Mountain Rescue
Covert Christmas
Payback
Christmas Undercover
Witness Pursuit
Mountain Ambush

Visit the Author Profile page at Harlequin.com.

NANNY WITNESS

HOPE WHITE

HARLEQUIN® LOVE INSPIRED® SUSPENSE

If you purchased this book without a cover you should be aware
that this book is stolen property. It was reported as "unsold and
destroyed" to the publisher, and neither the author nor the
publisher has received any payment for this "stripped book."

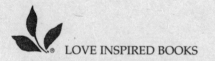

LOVE INSPIRED BOOKS

Recycling programs
for this product may
not exist in your area.

ISBN-13: 978-1-335-67906-2

Nanny Witness

Copyright © 2019 by Pat White

All rights reserved. Except for use in any review, the reproduction
or utilization of this work in whole or in part in any form by any
electronic, mechanical or other means, now known or hereafter
invented, including xerography, photocopying and recording, or in
any information storage or retrieval system, is forbidden without
the written permission of the editorial office, Love Inspired Books,
195 Broadway, New York, NY 10007 U.S.A.

This is a work of fiction. Names, characters, places and incidents are
either the product of the author's imagination or are used fictitiously, and
any resemblance to actual persons, living or dead, business establishments,
events or locales is entirely coincidental.

This edition published by arrangement with Love Inspired Books.

® and TM are trademarks of Love Inspired Books, used under license.
Trademarks indicated with ® are registered in the United States Patent
and Trademark Office, the Canadian Intellectual Property Office and in
other countries.

www.Harlequin.com

Printed in U.S.A.

Have not I commanded thee? Be strong and of a good courage; be not afraid, neither be thou dismayed: for the Lord thy God is with thee whithersoever thou goest.
–*Joshua* 1:9

This book is dedicated to my walking buddy,
Lynn Peterson, for her generous friendship.

ONE

Carly Winslow leaned over the white crib and stroked baby Mia's forehead.

"Such a good girl." Carly hummed a soft tune. As Mia's eyes drifted shut, the sound of a door slamming downstairs echoed through the baby monitor.

A moment later Mia's mom, Susan Bremerton, announced herself. "Hi, Carly, I'm home."

Carly grabbed the two-way device and said softly, "Hi, Mrs. B. Mia is taking a morning nap."

"Okay, thanks," Susan responded in a tone matching Carly's so as not to wake the baby.

Mia had drifted off and was sound asleep. She'd been fighting a cold and Mrs. B. had directed Carly to give Mia medicine to keep her comfortable.

Carly smiled as she watched the seven-month-old enjoy a peaceful, deep sleep, her little eyelids fluttering as she probably dreamed about the colorful animals on the mobile above her crib.

Crossing the room to a rocking chair, Carly picked up her notebook to study for her nurse's National Council licensure exam. She could go downstairs and make a cup of tea but decided against it. Carly had sensed tension lately in the home and she didn't want to intrude in Mrs. B.'s personal space.

She tucked her legs beneath her and thanked God for this wonderful job caring for the sweet baby girl an hour outside Denver in Miner, Colorado. Carly thought it would be good experience, and the salary would help her pay off school loans.

Ever since Carly started as Mia's nanny six months ago, she'd developed an attachment to the blond baby girl with the bright blue eyes. Even at a month old, Mia had a smile that lit up a room and warmed Carly's heart.

A smile that also triggered regret. The child was so vulnerable, which reminded Carly of her own utter failure—she should have done more to protect her little sister.

"Practice self-forgiveness." She whispered her aunt's advice and grabbed her notebook with review questions for the exam. Yet even now, at twenty-seven, Carly was plagued by a decision she'd made at the tender age of thirteen.

The sound of a door slamming echoed up the stairs. A few seconds of silence passed.

"Susan!" Mr. B.'s voice echoed through the monitor.

What was he doing home this time of day?

"What were you thinking?" Mr. B. said.

"I thought you'd be proud of me."

"Proud? About you destroying our lives?"

Uncomfortable that she was eavesdropping, Carly got up to turn down the monitor.

"What are you talking about?" Mrs. B. said. "It's a worthy project."

Loud pops cracked through the transmission.

Carly froze. It almost sounded like a car back-firing.

She stared at the white monitor for a second, wondering if the device was picking up sounds from another frequency. It had happened before.

"Harry!" Mrs. B. cried.

"Get down!"

Another pop echoed through the monitor. No, not a car backfiring. It sounded like…

Gunfire? That couldn't be right, not in this re-mote mansion with a solid security system.

"Calm, be calm," she coached herself.

Dashing across the room, Carly picked up Mia. There was no way she'd let any harm come to this child. Still asleep, Mia pressed her cheek against Carly's shoulder.

"Call 9-1-1!" Mr. B. shouted.

"I can't find my phone!"

"You can't hide from us," a male voice said.

Carly scanned the room. Should she take refuge in the closet? Then she'd be trapped if the shooter came upstairs.

The shooter. There was potentially a gunman in the house.

Her hands started to tremble. No, she was not that person. She'd given up fear and anxiety long ago, replacing it with faith and strength.

Strength she'd need to save Mia's life.

Clutching the baby firmly against her shoulder, she grabbed the monitor to keep tabs on the intruder's location and muted her side of the line. She cracked open the nursery door and slipped quietly into the hall.

"Harry!" Mrs. B.'s panicked voice cried.

Carly hurried into her room next door to Mia's and locked the door. That wouldn't stop a gunman, but it might slow him down long enough for Carly to escape onto her second-story porch and down the stairs to her car.

Carly felt an odd detachment to what was happening. Such detachment would make her a good nurse in a crisis, because she could distance herself and remain calm.

This situation wasn't about offering aid in a crisis. There was a gunman in the house and she needed help.

She grabbed her phone out of the side pocket of her purse.

Hesitated. Childhood trauma flooded her chest.

She had no choice. She had to call the police.

"Nine-one-one, what is your emergency?"

"I am at 536 Black Hawk Drive," Carly said. "Someone broke into the house and I heard gunfire."

"Gunfire?"

"I'm the nanny and I'm upstairs with the baby. I can hear it through the monitor."

"What is your name?"

"Carly—"

"Oh, no, you're hurt!" Mrs. B.'s voice cried through the monitor.

"Did you hear that?" Carly said to the operator.

"Officers are on the way, Carly. Please stay on the line."

Carly slipped the phone into the side pocket of her purse and flung it across her shoulder.

"Please, we have a baby," Mrs. B.'s voice said through the monitor.

Carly grabbed the soft baby carrier off her dresser and opened the porch door.

A crash and scream echoed through the monitor.

Keep going. Don't stop.

Carly crossed the small porch where she'd spend quiet nights reading and breathing in the crisp Colorado air. She glanced down at her car in the driveway. It was blocked by a black SUV. Time to come up with plan B.

As she descended the stairs, Carly eyed the forest in the distance. It was about a hundred yards away.

"Where is she?" a male voice shouted through the monitor.

"No," Mrs. B. cried. "Not the baby."

"Go get her."

A shiver pricked Carly's shoulders.

Carly placed the baby monitor on the stairs and pulled out her phone. "I'm taking the baby into the forest behind the house," she told the emergency operator.

As she jogged across the property with Mia in her arms, she prayed to God that the criminals weren't watching her from the picture windows spanning the back of the house.

"Such a good girl," she whispered against Mia's soft head of hair.

Closer. She was closing in on nature's refuge, perfect camouflage from the intruders.

Another muffled shot echoed across the property. She guessed they had reached her bedroom door and shot the lock open. They'd check the closet first, maybe under her bed. She had minutes, perhaps seconds, before they noticed the door leading to her private porch.

Carly dashed into the forest, following her favorite trail, the one she used for reflection on her daily Bible reading.

She never thought she'd use this trail to flee death.

"Hey!" a voice shouted.

Ignore it, she coached herself. No reason to panic about what might happen next.

Then she realized she'd be easy to follow if

she stayed on the trail, so she went rogue and ran deeper into the woods over juniper shrubs and sagebrush.

As she trudged farther into the mass of flora, she said a silent prayer.

Dear Lord, please help me protect this innocent child.

Another gunshot rang out, this one sounding like it was fired outside. Really? They thought shooting at her would convince her to stop running?

Adrenaline flooded her body. She ran faster, glancing over her shoulder only once. She broke through the mass of forest to a clearing.

And was looking below at a ten-foot drop to a riverbank. This was where she'd wait for help to arrive.

She laid Mia on the ground, adjusted the baby carrier around her own shoulders, picked up the child and strapped her in place across Carly's chest. Carly would need both hands to lower herself and Mia safely to the riverbank.

A sharp burst of wind chilled her to the core. Casting one last glance toward the Bremerton property, and seeing no one, she planned her descent. She kneeled and looked for a safe way down. A few rocks protruded from the side of the drop-off. That's where she'd plant her feet. Digging her fingers into the hard earth, she turned and got into position to lower herself.

The muted echo of sirens wailed in the far distance. Panic rushed through her, but she was no longer a child, no longer a part of that family. This time police might even help her.

If she could only remain invisible long enough for police to arrest the gunmen.

She lowered her right foot, still clinging to a rock at the edge of the cliff, her lifeline. Her foot steady on a rock below, she found another spot to hold on to, lowered her right hand and grabbed it.

Her foot slipped.

In what felt like slow motion, she fell, landing on the riverbank of rocks. Wind knocked from her lungs and she struggled to breathe, to think. Thoughts eluded her.

"Open your eyes," a deep male voice said.

How…how had the gunman reached her so quickly? Had she knocked her head and fallen unconscious?

She couldn't open her eyes, couldn't bear to see a gun pointed at her.

At Mia.

"No," she groaned.

"Let go of the baby."

Brody "Whit" Whittaker kneeled on the rocky shore next to the blond woman and child. He'd pulled up to his half brother's house and heard gunshots crack across the property.

What had Harry gotten himself into?

Whit covertly made his way onto the property and saw a young woman take off into the woods carrying a child, with a gunman trailing her. Whit followed them, hoping to protect the woman and child from the assailant.

"Ma'am, can you hear me?" Whit studied the fair-skinned, twentysomething woman, who clung to the child. Harry's child, Whit's half niece.

A child Whit hadn't met because of the complications of family.

"Ma'am—"

She gasp-coughed. "Don't touch her."

Although he heard a siren wailing in the distance, he knew it would take a few minutes before they arrived on the scene.

A lot could happen in a few minutes.

It sounded like the perps had already done some major damage, breaking into the house and potentially shooting his half brother and wife.

Whit had to shelve his panic over losing his brother and focus on protecting the baby and the woman clinging to her. Whit assumed she was the nanny, an innocent caught up in a mess. A mess of Harry's own making?

As a young man, Harry tended to make bad choices and refused to accept advice or help from his family. Whit and Harry had been estranged for more than ten years when Whit decided last fall it was time to mend things between them. He thought they were making progress, but after a few unreturned phone calls Whit grew worried that Harry was in trouble and was too proud to ask for help.

Whit followed his gut and decided to make an unannounced visit. Good thing he showed up when he did.

The baby squeaked. She was his blood, his family, and Whit wouldn't let anything happen to her.

Apparently, the nanny felt the same way.

"Ma'am, my name is Brody Whittaker. Harry Bremerton is my brother. You can trust me. I'm in town to visit Harry and I heard the gunshots. I'd like to help."

That got her to open her eyes. "Brother?"

"Yes, ma'am, half brother. I'm assuming you're the nanny?"

She nodded her affirmation. "He… I didn't know he had a brother."

Not surprising. Harry had kept his distance from Whit and the family, claiming they never understood or accepted him. Whit could see how Harry would get tired of the disapproving sighs and unwelcomed advice the family felt necessary to offer on a regular basis.

Whit cocked his head and thought he heard something. "We need to move. Okay?"

She still didn't seem like she trusted him. Understandable. She'd no doubt experienced a violent and traumatic attack. Her adrenaline must be pounding like water hitting the rocks at the bottom of Jasper Falls.

"I'm not sure what to say to convince you I'm one of the good guys," he started. "I noticed a small boat down the shoreline. We can use that to get away."

She closed her eyes. That couldn't be good, Whit thought. Then her lips moved slightly as if she was whispering to herself.

He pushed aside the thought that any second now a gunman would peer below and pick them off like cans on a split rail fence.

"Ma'am—"

"Please help me up," she said, opening her eyes.

This time he couldn't help but notice the remarkable blend of colors: green, gold and brown.

"Would you like me to carry the baby?"

She put out her hand. "No, thank you."

With a nod, he offered his good arm and helped her stand. When she wavered, he gripped her shoulders to keep her vertical. He quickly released her since it was obvious his right-handed grip was weaker than his left.

Someday, they'd said. *Eventually*. Or maybe never.

She squinted, as if studying him, trying to make out what he was thinking.

"This way." He led her down the riverbank away from Harry's property and hopefully from danger. "The baby is awfully good."

"Yes, she's a very sweet girl." The nanny kissed the top of Mia's head.

The nanny. He realized he didn't know her name.

"You can call me Whit, and your name is…?"

"Carly." She hesitated before sharing her last name. "Winslow."

"Good to meet you, Carly Winslow. Unfortunate circumstances."

"You…you heard the gunfire coming from the Bremerton house?" she said.

"Yes."

"You don't seem all that upset about your brother."

"I'm in cop mode."

"Oh."

She sounded disappointed.

He glanced over his shoulder; he saw no one following them on the riverbank.

"I'm still wondering why I've never heard of you," Carly said.

She was cautious, a good trait for a nanny.

"Truth is—" he hesitated "—Harry and I have a conflicted relationship."

"Oh, I'm sorry," she said.

So was Whit. Some mistakes you never shook off.

"Where are the rest of the police officers?" she said.

"Not here yet."

"Then how did you find me?" She stopped suddenly.

He read concern in her eyes. "I'm not lying to you, Carly."

"So where are the rest of the cops?"

"I'm not with local law enforcement. I'm on temporary leave from the Dallas PD."

"On leave? For what?" Her eyes narrowed with suspicion.

"Injured in the line of duty. Still recovering."

He motioned for her to walk with him. She didn't move.

"I don't think it's a good idea to wait for local deputies when we've got a gunman trailing us, do you?"

She nodded, and they continued to the boat. He held it steady so she could climb in. Again, he was about to offer to hold the baby, when he realized she was securely strapped against Carly in a carrying device. Once Carly and the child were settled, Whit pushed the boat into the water and jumped in. He rowed, steering them parallel to the riverbank, not wanting to drift too far out and expose their location.

The baby stirred, and Carly managed to soothe her by humming a soft tune.

They floated south and Whit scanned the area for a decent spot to pull over and take cover. The piercing wail of sirens grew louder. Relief eased the tension in his shoulders.

The crack of a gunshot rang out.

"Get down!" he ordered Carly.

Whit rowed faster but could do only so much with the limited mobility of his right arm. Where was the gunfire coming from?

He leaned left and spotted a man racing down the shoreline in pursuit. Whit couldn't row and shoot at the same time and didn't have confidence that he'd hit his mark with his left hand anyway.

A second shot nicked the side of the boat. As Whit rowed faster, the usual dull ache up his right arm grew to a pulsating throb. Not an entirely bad thing since the pain would keep him sharp.

They passed a six-foot metal fence separating two properties. The assailant would have to scale the fence or dive into the river and swim after them. Whit kept rowing, waiting for the perfect opportunity to offload the woman and child so he could give them cover.

With every stroke of the oars, his head ached and his arm throbbed. The assailant ran up against the fence and started climbing.

The current carried the small boat downstream. Whit dug the oar into the left side and they swung to shore.

"Get out," he said.

Carly didn't move. Had she been hit?

He pulled the boat ashore. "Carly?"

She glanced up, her colorful eyes brimming with fear. The baby whimpered against her and instinct made Whit want to pull them both against his chest to protect them, calm them.

Yeah, who was he kidding?

"Take the baby up those stairs to safety." He pointed to wooden steps. "Tell the police you're about a mile south of the Bremerton property." Not waiting for her response, he helped her out of the boat and tipped it on its side. He withdrew his gun and waited, balancing his left hand on his right palm to steady his shot. Out of the corner of his eye he saw Carly still standing there.

"Go!" he ordered, and her shoulders jerked. She turned and headed up the stairs.

Whit eyed the gunman. The perp climbed the fence and dropped down to the shoreline. Although a clumsy fall, he regained his balance and marched straight for Whit. Whit cast one last glance over his shoulder. Carly and the baby were out of sight. Good, he hadn't failed them.

"Come on out of there!" the gunman shouted.

The rowboat served as decent cover but wouldn't stop a bullet.

"I just want the kid!"

Whit leaned the barrel of his gun against the front end of the boat, inhaled a slow, deep breath and took his shot.

TWO

A gunshot cracked through the air. Carly gasped and jogged faster.

"Breathe," she whispered to herself. She didn't want to trip and fall because she was in a frantic state. She had to shove aside the fear pulsing through her body and get to safety.

What about the man who'd helped her? She hoped the bad guys hadn't shot him.

Bad guys. They might have shot Mr. and Mrs. B. and now were after the baby. Well, they weren't getting anywhere near sweet Mia as long as Carly was here to protect her. Carly might not be a martial arts expert or know how to handle a gun, but she was a fighter to her core.

Carly was the only thing standing between violent criminals and the innocent child strapped to her chest. Not entirely true. She wasn't the only thing standing in their way. There was Mr. B.'s half brother, Whit.

Mr. and Mrs. Bremerton rarely mentioned extended family, nor had Mr. B. mentioned his handsome brother.

Handsome? Where had that come from? Must be the trauma of the past twenty minutes that had her noticing things like his warm blue eyes, eyes that radiated truth when he said she could trust him.

She knew better. He was a cop, and cops couldn't be trusted.

As she crossed the well-manicured back lawn, she realized how exposed she was out here in the open. Carly spotted a shed. It was closer than the multimillion-dollar home in the distance, so she opted for a quick duck-and-cover.

When she approached the shed, she noted there was no lock on the door. She breathed a sigh of relief. Then she wondered if she was being watched by security cameras on the property. Couldn't think about that now. Needed to hide long enough for police to rescue her.

Darting into the shed, she found a spot on the floor beside a large riding lawn mower. There were quite a few tools stored in the shed—hoes, rakes and shovels—along with jugs of gasoline. Although not the safest place for a baby, it was better than being out in the open, exposed to a gunman.

Kissing Mia's head, she thanked God that the child was such a good sleeper. Even with all the jostling and juggling, Mia didn't fuss much. Carly pulled out her phone and called Emergency again.

"It's Carly Winslow. I escaped the Bremerton house and I'm about a mile south of the property. The gunman is still after us. A man named Brody Whittaker helped me—"

The shed door flung open.

Carly gasped.

"Get out of there," said a large man looming in the doorway.

Her heart pounded against her chest and fear kept her frozen in place.

The gunman stepped inside the shed.

"I'm coming, I'm coming." She slipped her phone into her pocket and stood awkwardly, clutching Mia.

The guy moved out of the shed and turned his back on Carly, assuming she wasn't a threat.

No matter how frightened she was, Carly Anna Winslow was not a quitter and she surely wasn't going to let this man take or harm Mia. She snatched a shovel and just as he turned...

She swung with all her strength.

Unfortunately, she missed his head and nailed him in the shoulder, which seemed only to irritate him.

Reaching out with huge hands, he grabbed the metal head of the shovel and yanked. She stumbled forward and let go so she wouldn't be pulled against the creep's body.

He tossed the shovel aside, at least ten feet away, took a few steps back and withdrew his weapon. Mia was strapped to Carly's chest, which meant if he fired he'd hit the baby. Carly instinctively spun around, turning her back to the attacker. She dropped to her knees and hugged Mia.

"Give me the kid!"

There was no way she'd willingly hand over this child.

"Let's go, now!"

Carly rocked Mia and softly sang to her.

"I'll shoot!" he threatened.

She heard grunting and a shot rang out.

She gasped.

Didn't feel anything.

The bullet hadn't hit her.

"Praise God," Carly whispered.

Mia burst into tears, the sound of the gunshot having frightened her.

They were alive. Either that or Carly imagined heaven just like this, with a child in her arms.

"Carly, are you okay?"

She glanced up. Brody Whittaker stood above her wearing a concerned frown, blood seeping from a cut on his head.

"I'm… Yes?" she said. It came out as a question because the definition of *okay* was muddled at this point.

"The baby?" he asked.

"She's okay, too."

"Good." He sighed.

She noticed more blood staining his jacket.

"Have you been shot?"

"I'll be fine. Let's go." He offered his hand.

She took it and he helped her up. He blocked her view of the attacker, who lay sprawled on the ground.

"Keep your eyes trained forward," Whit said.

With an absent nod, she followed his instructions and looked away. "Did you shoot him?"

"No, he took my gun, so I nailed him pretty hard with the shovel."

In the distance, two sheriff's deputies sprinted into the backyard. "Hands where I can see 'em!" one shouted.

Fear skittered across her shoulders. She shoved it back. This was no time to let childhood trauma dictate her behavior.

"Do as they ask and everything will be fine," Whit said.

She had a hard time believing him. In her experience things went very bad very quickly where police were concerned.

Even if you were innocent.

"I'm a police officer," Whit identified himself, raising his hands.

"On your knees! Hands up!" the second deputy said.

Carly hesitated.

"Hands!" the deputy repeated.

Her heart rate sped up.

"They don't know what they just walked into," Whit said. "It'll be fine." With a nod, he lowered himself to his knees, encouraging her to do the same. "Keep your hands where they can see them."

She did as ordered, although every instinct cried out that she should cradle the baby. Lowering her gaze to the green lawn, Carly wondered how long she'd have to remain in this subservient position.

You'll sit here until you tell us the truth.

Carly shoved the memory aside. This was different. She wasn't being punished…well, not exactly.

"I… I'm sorry you got pulled into all this," Whit said.

She glanced at him. "It's not your fault."

"I just…wanted…" He blinked his bloodshot eyes a few times and collapsed.

Harry Bremerton struggled to breathe through the pain of a throbbing head injury. The tight blindfold didn't help. He reached for it.

"If you take off your blindfold, you're dead."

As if Harry and Susan weren't already dead.

Harry couldn't think that way, wouldn't give up so easily. He needed to negotiate with their kidnappers, or at least buy some time.

"If this is about—"

"I didn't give you permission to talk!" the kidnapper shouted.

Susan whimpered, and Harry pulled her close.

Was this a kidnapping for ransom? Who'd pay it? His mother and stepdad did okay but they weren't nearly as wealthy as Harry, and Harry's brother, Whit, was just a cop.

"Okay, you may speak," the kidnapper said.

"Please, my daughter is sick," Susan said. "She needs us."

Their kidnapper didn't respond.

"I have money," Harry said.

Maniacal laughter echoed off the walls, sending a chill down Harry's spine.

"Where is the child?" the kidnapper said.

Stunned, Harry didn't answer. Why did they care about Mia? Were they going to use her to manipulate him? Control him?

Suddenly Susan was being pulled away. Harry held on to her.

"Stop, please, wait!" Harry shouted.

"Who has the child?"

"I assume Carly, our nanny."

The kidnapper released Susan and she curled up against Harry's chest, sobbing.

"What's Carly's last name?"

"Winslow."

"Where does she live?"

Buy time.

"At our house."

"Where would she go if she couldn't be at your house?"

Harry had no idea. Between her nanny responsibilities and studying for her nursing exam, she didn't have much of a social life.

Something jabbed his ribs, sending a sharp pain through his body.

"I don't know. I really don't," he croaked.

Harry feared that was the wrong answer. It was the only one he had.

Was this it? The last moments of his life? Regret tore through him for many things, especially for the resentment he'd carried around for years.

Regret for not making peace with his brother.

The next few, torturous minutes seemed to stretch like hours. Harry held his wife tight.

Please, God, he prayed, because during the course of their marriage he'd grown to accept the concept of a higher power. He'd opened his heart to God.

A door clicked shut. He wasn't sure how much time had passed when he finally felt bold enough to peek out from beneath the blindfold.

He and Susan were alone.

Whit struggled to remain conscious. Pain seared down his arm as if someone held a branding iron against his skin.

Suddenly he was back in the dark alley lying in a pool of his own blood. Was this it? Was this how it was going to end, with Whit alone and bleeding out in a foul-smelling alley having done nothing substantial with his life? The thought made him fight back, fight harder than he thought possible.

"Brody, open your eyes," a woman said.

A woman, not his partner, Tina. She'd never call him by his given name.

"He's stable," another female said.

Stable? More like unstable and disabled. For life.

"Ma'am, I'm going to have to ask you to release the child," a man said.

"I'd rather not."

Whit recognized her voice. He fought the urge to drift off to sleep.

"The child isn't yours, and it's not his," the man said. "Which is why you need to relinquish her to the state."

"Absolutely not."

The edge to her voice sounded more than determined. It sounded threatening.

"If I have to arrest you, I will," the man said.

Whit groaned and willed his eyes to open. Talk about a crowd. One guy, obviously a cop, stood at the foot of his bed, a woman Whit guessed was a doctor stood next to him, and on Whit's left was a nurse in colorful scrubs. Then Whit slowly turned to his right.

There stood the woman he'd rescued from his brother's house and she still clung to Whit's niece.

What was the woman's name again? Carly, that's right. The nanny.

Carly was glaring at the cop. "Brody Whittaker is the child's uncle and he should decide what happens next with the baby. I'm not surrendering Mia to the foster care system when her uncle is right here and perfectly capable of taking custody."

All eyes focused on Whit. He wanted to puff out his chest, sit up in bed, something. His arm still burned. He clenched his jaw against the pain, not wanting to wince and expose his weakness. Carly was right. The child shouldn't be sent into temporary foster care, especially with a potential threat still out there.

The threat. Someone was after Whit's niece and Whit had bashed the guy's head with the shovel before he could shoot Carly. Whit would've shot him if the guy hadn't taken his piece.

"Brody, I'm Dr. Monroe," the woman with short red hair said. "You have a bullet wound, a head injury and a concussion. How is the pain on a scale from one to ten?"

"About a three," he fudged. "What about the assailant?" he asked.

"He's in custody. I'm Detective Harper with the Summit County Sheriff's Office," the cop, mid-forties, introduced himself.

"My weapon?"

"The hospital has secured it until you're released." Harper glanced at the others. "Can I get a few minutes alone with Detective Whittaker?"

Okay, so Harper must have checked with the Dallas PD to confirm Whit's identity.

The nurse in colorful scrubs placed the call button beside Whit's hand. "Use this if you need anything."

She and the doctor left. Carly, the nanny, did not.

"Would you…?" Harper motioned for Carly to leave.

"I'd rather she stays," Whit said.

Harper eyed him. Whit could tell he wanted to say something cop-to-cop but held back.

"Could you help us piece together what happened today?" Harper said.

"Someone broke into the house and shot Mr. and Mrs. Bremerton, that's what happened," Carly said in a defiant tone.

"Ma'am, I'm speaking to Detective Whittaker."

Whit looked at Carly, who wore a protective expression on her face.

"It's okay," Whit said to her. "Let's talk this through."

She nodded. Didn't look pleased.

Whit redirected his attention to Harper. "I went to visit my brother and heard gunshots."

"Do you visit your brother often?"

Guilt sparked inside his chest. "Not often, no.

He hadn't returned a few phone calls, so I decided to check on him."

"From Dallas."

"Yes."

"Which meant you were worried about him. Why?"

How could Whit explain that?

"I don't know, gut instinct?" That and Harry had a way of getting into trouble, at least as a teenager. "Besides, I hadn't met my niece yet." He shot a slight smile toward Mia.

"Were you inside the Bremerton home at the time of the break-in?" Harper asked.

"No. When I got to the property, the gates were open, which I thought was odd. Once on the grounds I heard gunshots and decided to investigate. That's when I saw Carly fleeing the scene."

"Fleeing?"

"Bad word choice," Whit said. "Escaping, with my niece in her arms. A tall man, dressed in black, was in pursuit. He fired off a warning shot and she kept running. I saw her disappear into the forest and followed."

"The man in black didn't follow her?"

"He kept to the trail. She did not. Nor did I."

"Then what happened?"

"I helped Carly and the baby into a boat and we went downstream. The perp followed us on foot. I sent Carly to what I thought was safety, but the perp—" Whit hesitated, not wanting to admit this part "—overpowered me and went after her." Whit glanced at Carly. "Didn't you give him your statement?"

"I did," Carly said with a lift of her chin.

"I'd like to hear your version," Harper said, nodding at Whit.

"I regained consciousness and climbed up to the property. I knocked the guy out just as he was about to shoot Carly. That's when deputies arrived."

Harper directed his attention to Carly. "Would you care to fill in any blanks, Miss—" he hesitated "—Winslow?"

"That accurately describes what happened after the break-in."

"You have no idea who broke in to the Bremerton home?"

"As I said before, I was upstairs. I heard gunshots through the monitor and called 9-1-1."

"And left the premises," Harper said. "You didn't consider waiting for police?"

"Wait where? They had guns. They shot Mr. and Mrs. Bremerton."

"So, they did shoot my brother?" Whit said.

"There's no evidence of that," Harper said.

"I heard it through the baby monitor," Carly said. "I heard Mrs. B. screaming her husband's name and said he was hurt."

"And you ran," Harper said, accusation in his tone.

Carly clenched her jaw tight.

"Because what, you changed your mind about kidnapping the kid?"

"Excuse me?" Carly said. "They tried to kill me, too, just like the Bremertons."

"Back up, they killed my brother?" Whit said, struggling to control his panic.

Harper shook his head. "No one was killed today. When we got to the house it was empty, ransacked and shot up pretty good, but empty. The Bremertons weren't home. So…" He looked at Carly. Waited.

"I know what I heard through the monitor," Carly said.

"That your final answer?" Harper pressed.

"Hey, ease up," Whit said, having developed an inexplicable need to protect Carly Winslow. Maybe not so inexplicable considering she'd saved his niece's life. "The guy who was shooting at us was very real."

"Yeah, well, I'm wondering if this was a burglary-kidnapping gone wrong. The nanny had a change of heart and the guy came after her."

"Wait, you think I—"

"You're basing that on what, exactly?" Whit interrupted Carly.

The cop looked Whit straight in the eye. "The fact that the nanny has a record."

And there it was, Carly's past rising to destroy any chance she had at a normal life. She didn't miss the dimming of Brody Whittaker's eyes, or how his expression changed from protective to skeptical. She thought she even read betrayal.

Shame flooded her chest, making her feel three feet tall, like that confused child. The trauma burned raw and painful, and so very real.

She was thirteen again, being questioned by police. Feeling bullied, shamed and, worst of all, abandoned by her parents.

"Carly?"

She glanced at Whit, who looked like he expected her to explain herself, proclaim her innocence. She couldn't lie. She had, in fact, broken the law, thinking she was doing so to protect her baby sister, Greta. Only years later, as an adult, did Carly truly understand what had happened. Carly's parents could be so convincing, so manipulative. Mother was especially a master at it.

"Yes, I have a record." Carly glanced at Detective Harper. "From when I was thirteen. And it's expunged."

"Which doesn't mean it didn't happen," Harper said.

A shudder trickled across her shoulders. It was

just a matter of time before the wound would be ripped open again, and Whit found out the truth.

"Okay, something's not making sense here," Whit said. "Did my brother know you had a record?"

"He did," she said.

"Yet he hired you to take care of his child."

Right, because someone who'd been tricked into making a horrible mistake at thirteen years old wasn't redeemable. Bad was bad. Forever. Or so many people believed.

Thankfully Carly's aunt Vicky had taken Carly in with a warm and compassionate heart at a time when Carly could have drifted deeper into the darkness. Aunt Vicky believed in second chances, in the power of prayer and healing. She believed in Carly, and challenged her to believe in herself. With the help of her aunt and God, Carly had found a modicum of peace.

"Miss Winslow?" the detective pushed. "Or should I say Miss Garber?"

"You changed your name?" Whit said, suspicion coloring his voice.

How could she explain that she didn't want any connection with the criminals who were her biological parents?

"Yes, I changed my name," she said. "I met Mr. and Mrs. Bremerton when I was working for Palace Catering. They were at a party and—"

"Wait, you worked private parties?" the detective asked. "In people's homes?"

Carly straightened. "Just because there was an incident when I was thirteen doesn't mean I'm a violent criminal as an adult."

"So you're admitting your crime was a violent one?" Detective Harper jotted something in his notebook.

She ignored the detective's question and looked at Whit. "I'd been hired to serve at a party. Mrs. Bremerton was having an anxiety attack and I helped keep her calm until paramedics arrived."

The detective seemed skeptical. Whit, however, looked interested, as if he wanted to hear more.

"Later that year, the Bremertons tracked me down and asked if I'd consider being Mia's nanny," Carly continued. "I explained my situation, that I was finishing up nursing school. They offered me a generous salary, and the baby was so sweet." She kissed the top of Mia's head and glanced at Whit. "That's when I told them about my past, how I made a mistake when I was thirteen. They knew what happened and offered me the job anyway."

"You want to tell us what you were charged with?" Detective Harper asked.

Keep your mouth shut. Don't share too much or they'll use it against you.

"Not at this time," she said.

"You told the Bremertons," he pressed.

"Because we were about to enter into a relationship where I'd be living at their house, like a member of the family."

"But you aren't family, and this isn't your child," Detective Harper said.

"I'm perfectly aware of that." His statement burned, especially since she'd felt like a member of the Bremerton household for the past six months.

On cue, Mia woke up and squirmed in Carly's arms. She wanted to be fed, and Carly had nothing to give her.

"The child needs to be checked out by a doctor," the detective said to Whit. "Miss Winslow is refusing to let us do that."

"Mia isn't hurt. I've kept her safe." Carly looked at Whit. "If you'd like a doctor to examine her, that's fine. Since you were unconscious, I feared they would take her away and put her into the foster care system. I didn't think that was the best thing for Mia." Carly gently rocked with the child to calm her.

Whit pressed the call button and a moment later the nurse entered the room. "I'd like a doctor to take a look at my niece to see if she's okay."

Her grip tightened around Mia. Carly still feared the child would be taken away, that she'd never see her again.

Like Greta.

With a heavy heart, Carly kissed the top of Mia's head, unhooked her from the carrier and passed her to the nurse. "She's probably hungry. She drinks soy-based formula."

The nurse nodded and left the room with Mia.

Carly glanced out the window at the Colorado sky, gray, like her mood. She unstrapped the baby carrier from her body and slowly placed it on the chair. Sadness consumed her.

It was over. Her fresh start as a nanny, being able to shower Mia with oodles of love Carly had stored up for years, love she'd wanted to lavish on her baby sister.

"I'd like you to come with me, Miss Winslow," the detective said.

Carly sighed. She should have known that was coming.

"No, thank you," she said politely.

"No, thank you? What kind of answer is that?"

"I'm not leaving the hospital until I'm relieved of my duties." She turned to Whit. His brows furrowed in a puzzled expression.

"Since the Bremertons are missing and I'm Mia's nanny, that makes you my temporary employer," she said to him. "Therefore, I'll stay until you release me."

"Miss Winslow—"

"You have no cause to arrest me," she interrupted Detective Harper. "Just because I have a juvenile record does not mean I'm a criminal. Besides, I protected Mia."

The detective shook his head.

"It's true," Whit confirmed. "She did protect my niece."

She breathed a sigh of relief. Whit appreciated that there was more to Carly than her past.

"However," Whit continued, holding her gaze, "Detective Harper could use your help with the investigation about what happened today."

In other words, Whit was dismissing her from duty into the hands of a bully.

"Bring Carly back when you're done, Detective," Whit said. "I'll need her help with the baby when I'm released."

Sure. Whatever. They all knew she wasn't returning to the hospital, that she'd never see Mia or Whit again.

Go live with Aunt Vicky for a while. We'll send for you in a couple of months. Everything will be okay.

Everything wasn't okay. Her parents didn't send for her. Her mom didn't even call or write. Worse, they eventually moved without giving Carly a forwarding address.

She stepped up to Whit's bedside and placed her hand on his arm. "It's been an honor taking care of Mia. She's a precious little girl. May the Lord protect you both."

With a weak smile, she turned and walked out of the room.

* * *

The kidnappers left a few water bottles and a box of crackers in the room where they kept Harry and Susan.

The room. Their prison. Harry wished they'd get on with it, make their ransom demands. He prayed that Mia and Carly were safe. There was something about Carly, a kind of strength and determination that made him choose her for the job as nanny.

The lock clicked on the door.

"Keep the blindfold on." He shifted Susan's blindfold in place and did the same with his own.

"Mr. Bremerton," the kidnapper said. "Do you have any idea what it feels like to have everything taken from you?"

Not quite, but Harry had suffered loss in his life. It seemed like he wasn't done suffering.

"I know, yes," Harry said.

"What have you lost, you arrogant, entitled prince?"

That's when Harry realized nothing he said would appease this man.

"I want to help you," Harry said.

"How generous. Isn't he generous? I'll bet he's a good father. Are you a good father?"

"I'd like to think so."

"Do you think Mia misses you?"

The image of her sweet face tore at Harry's insides.

"Does the little girl cry for her papa?" the man

said, closer now, as if he was trying to get inside Harry's head.

"Papa, where's my papa?" He mimicked a child's voice.

"What do you want?" Harry ground out.

Then Harry had a horrible thought: What if they hurt Susan to punish him for his sharp tone? Harry held her close.

"I was taught never to lay a hand on a woman," the man said. "I was beaten when I slapped my sister."

Too bad the guy's parents didn't teach him it wasn't right to kidnap and torment strangers.

Footsteps tapped against the floor as the man crossed the room.

"No one takes what is mine. You will spend the rest of your life suffering for your mistake."

A few hours later, Whit struggled to put on his clothes at the hospital. It wasn't easy with one semifunctional arm and the other still throbbing from a gunshot wound. He could have used Carly's help right about now, yet he'd sent her away, into the lion's den, to be questioned by police.

Carly, the nanny with a criminal record. A juvenile record. Would her past show a pattern of behavior, or had she made a stupid kid's mistake? He'd seen plenty of those in his years on the force, and he'd also seen plenty of crimes that indicated a consistent pattern of behavior.

He managed to get his jeans on and dug into the bag for his shirt. He hesitated as he remembered Carly's fierceness while protecting baby Mia. That was not rehearsed or fake. Love shone in her eyes when she looked at the child, when she hugged and kissed Mia. Whit might be aloof; however, he knew what love looked like.

You couldn't help but read every emotion that crossed Carly's face. She wore it all out there, like a book with words in extra-large print. Unless you were consumed by procedure and protocol, blinded by suspicion, which Whit normally would be if he were on the job.

Today he was a brother and an uncle. He'd let the cops do their job and he'd do his: protect his niece.

Harry, where are you? Detective Harper said they weren't at the mansion when police arrived, which meant they'd been kidnapped.

Whit decided to call his brother in the hopes he'd escaped somehow and needed help. His call went into voice mail.

"Hey, it's Brody. I hope you're okay, man. We're all worried about you. Your daughter's safe. She's in my custody until you return. The nanny is helping to make sure Mia's okay, because…well, we both know I'm not the best caregiver in the world. Anyway, call me."

He slipped the phone into his denim jacket,

ignoring the now brown bloodstain where he'd been shot.

"Hey, where are you going?" a nurse asked, stepping into his room.

"Hospitals aren't my thing."

"Let's at least sling that arm." The nurse helped adjust the sling around his shoulder. "What's the hurry?"

"I've got a baby girl to take care of."

"She's fine. Her aunt Judy is here."

Whit froze. "Who?"

"Aunt Judy, from Boulder?"

"She doesn't have an aunt Judy."

THREE

"Where's Mia?" Whit asked the nurse.

"First floor, Pediatrics."

He rushed out of the room to the stairs and headed down two flights to the main floor. There was no one named Judy in his entire extended family. Then again, maybe he was overreacting and Judy was from his sister-in-law's side. How could anyone know about today's break-in at the house and the disappearance of his half brother and his wife? Whit hadn't had a chance to contact family.

The stitches burned as he descended the stairs a little too aggressively, his thoughts consumed by needing to get to his niece before she disappeared. Okay, so maybe a small part of him believed what the detective was selling, that Carly was a part of this, that she'd gotten herself involved in a kidnapping-for-ransom scheme. Nursing school had to be expensive, right?

If Harry had offered a generous nanny salary,

why would she risk being caught in a criminal act, especially with her background? *Once a criminal always a criminal.*

Deep in his gut that conclusion felt wrong, inconsistent with the protective and nurturing young woman he'd met today.

He followed signs to Pediatrics, shoved open the door and spotted a nurse. "Mia Bremerton?" he demanded.

The nurse caught sight of the bloodstain on his jacket and hesitated.

"She's about this big." He motioned with his hands, because he wasn't sure of her age. "Blond hair? Her aunt supposedly came for her."

"Oh, they just left."

"*Just*, as in seconds, minutes, what?"

"Maybe a minute ago?"

He spun around and headed toward the main entrance. Would a kidnapper use that entrance to flee? Sure, if she was pretending to be a member of the family she could casually stroll out the front door.

"Sir, is there a problem?" a security officer questioned.

"Someone kidnapped my niece."

The officer jogged up beside him and they went outside. Whit scanned the parking lot across the street.

The sound of a baby crying raised the hair on the back of his neck. He spotted a woman in a long tan jacket juggling a fussy Mia while opening the car door.

Without thinking, Whit started to take off.

A car horn blared.

The guard gripped Whit's jacket and yanked him back, just as a service truck whizzed by. The driver made a face at Whit like he was an idiot.

He'd be a lot worse than an idiot if his niece got taken on his watch.

"Stop!" the guard shouted as they crossed the street.

Whit wished the guard hadn't alerted the kidnapper to their presence. She slammed the back door and got behind the wheel. Did she even strap his niece into a car seat?

They were about a hundred feet away when she shoved it into gear and took off, peeling across the parking lot, nearly hitting a car as she made a sharp turn.

"You get the plates?" the guard said.

"Yep."

She sped up to the exit.

They chased after her.

Whit automatically reached for his gun and remembered the hospital still had it.

"My truck's over here," the security guard said. Whit kept his eyes on the white minivan that was nearing the exit gate.

Whit and the guard climbed into his truck. The guard pulled out and Whit called Emergency.

"A child's been abducted from Saint Mary's Hospital. Tell Detective Harper it's Mia Bremerton. The suspect is female, Caucasian, dark hair, about five foot eight. She drove off in a white minivan."

He gave them the plate number and watched the van turn onto the main road. Whit didn't want this to become a high-speed chase, putting Mia at even more risk.

He had to get her back.

The little girl was family and he was responsible for her.

"Give her space," Whit said to the security guard.

"I don't want to lose them," he said.

"I know, but we don't want to force her into making a bad driving decision either."

The guard nodded in agreement.

"I'm Brody Whittaker, by the way."

"Steve Meyers. Didn't expect to be chasing a kidnapper when I came into work today. Why did she take your niece?"

"Don't know." This entire day had been filled with questions and no answers, Whit thought.

One answer was obviously clear: Mia needed her uncle to protect her from whatever his brother may have gotten himself into. Whit shouldn't assume this was about Harry, yet it wouldn't surprise him. Harry tended to take risks, risks that could have led to putting his baby girl in danger.

Maybe if Whit had stayed around longer, been a good role model for his brother growing up, Harry would have turned out more grounded. It was obvious that Whit's stepdad didn't have much time for his son.

Instead Whit took off after high school, joined the army and kept his distance from his mom, half brother and half sister, Beth. He thought he'd made that decision out of respect for the family. Recently he began to wonder if shame had driven him away.

Shame that he'd been so utterly selfish as a teenager. He hadn't prevented Harry from getting hurt.

Ever since Whit's brush with death on the job, he'd been determined to heal his relationship with Harry. Whit wanted to be a good brother, and a loving uncle to Mia.

"She's turning onto Mountain Pass drive," Steve said.

"Is that a bad thing?"

"Narrow road. Sharp turns."

Whit relayed the information to the 9-1-1 operator.

"I'm sending deputies to intercept her," the operator said.

"Thanks." Whit turned to Steve. "Let's not crowd her." He certainly didn't want her rolling the van with his niece in the back seat.

Whit's eyes burned as he stared ahead at the

kidnapper's vehicle. They would lose the white minivan to a sharp turn, and then catch sight of it again. It was awfully bold of the kidnapper to walk into a hospital, pretend to be a family member and leave with the child.

Bold and criminal.

"She won't get far," Steve said, trying to make Whit feel better.

Steve approached a sharp turn a little too fast and they came dangerously close to skidding off into a ravine.

"Sorry, I'll slow it down," he said.

Whit nodded, his vocal cords tied into knots. He used to love the adrenaline rush, the buzz of a chase, although not when it involved one of his own, and there were very few of those left in his life. His serious romantic relationships couldn't withstand his commitment to the job, and he'd grown distant from his work family because of his medical leave.

He found himself at an impasse, possibly forced to sit behind a desk for the rest of his career. It wasn't the same as being out in the field, of leading an investigation. He wasn't sure what the future held professionally, what he'd end up doing.

That untethered feeling made him realize how important it was to have a support system, a real family. He and his half sister, Beth, had reconnected, and he thought he was on the right track with Harry, until he'd stopped returning Whit's calls.

"Where'd she go?" Steve peered out the window.

"Down on the right?" Whit craned his neck, hoping to see the minivan.

They reached a four-way stop and looked both directions.

The minivan, with his niece in the back seat, was gone.

Never talk to police, her mother's voice whispered in the recesses of her mind. The family code.

By now Carly should want nothing to do with her family, their advice, their lies. Yet childhood trauma was imprinted on her heart.

If you talk to police, they will take Greta away.

Carly readjusted her position in the interrogation room chair and crossed her arms over her chest. She was proud of herself for remaining calm and not allowing her past to cause her to have a total meltdown. After all, the last time she'd been questioned by police she was a naive thirteen-year-old who'd been played by her mother and cajoled by authorities.

No one had cared about Carly's well-being. They all had their own agendas: her parents wanted her gone and the cops wanted to finish their paperwork.

Still, when Carly stepped into this room with the one table and chairs on either side, the past flashed through her mind.

The fight with her mother.

Hiding Greta in her room to protect her.

Police breaking down the door. *Put down the knife.*

"So, you've been employed by the Bremertons for six months?" Detective Harper asked.

"Yes, since the baby was a month old."

Harper had asked that twice already.

"And the vehicle you saw blocking your car was a dark SUV?"

That was the third time he'd asked that one.

"Yes."

"You couldn't see the plate numbers?"

She was done with this irritating line of questioning. She assumed he was stalling until he could somehow get more information about her juvenile crime.

"Shouldn't you be looking for Mr. and Mrs. B.?"

"Maybe if you gave me more information it would help me find them."

Right, keep her talking until she said something he could use against her. She knew how it worked.

"Detective, I have been chased, shot at and assaulted," Carly said. "I'm tired and would like to leave now."

Harper shot her a displeased look, but she

wouldn't be intimidated. She wasn't that thirteen-year-old girl, scared, alone and charged with felony menacing because she'd been trying to protect her little sister.

"I've answered your questions. Am I free to go?" she pushed.

"You haven't answered the most critical one—what were you charged with when you were thirteen?"

She clenched her jaw and stared at the door behind him. Giving Harper that piece of her history would convince him she was guilty of something, anything. Today she was guilty only of loving and wanting to protect baby Mia.

"Lawyer, please," she said.

Harper's eye twitched.

A young deputy in his twenties popped his head into the room. "Detective, an emergency call just came in. A child's been abducted from Saint Mary's Hospital."

Carly stood. "Mia?"

Detective Harper turned to her. "What do you know about this?"

"What could I possibly know? I've been in here with you."

He narrowed his eyes as if assessing her honesty. Finally, he said, "You're free to go. Not back to the Bremerton estate. It's a crime scene."

"My car's there, and my clothes."

He nodded at the young deputy. "Schneider,

give Miss Winslow a ride to her car and make sure she vacates the premises without taking anything from the house." Harper turned back to Carly. "I'd prefer you not leave Summit County."

Oh, she had no plans to leave the county or even the small town of Miner, Colorado. Carly wasn't going anywhere until she knew Mia was safe.

"Ma'am." The young deputy motioned.

She accompanied the deputy and left the police station, hopefully never to return.

Twenty minutes later Deputy Schneider pulled up the long driveway of the Bremerton estate. The gates, which were usually closed, were wide open to allow access to law enforcement officials. Carly felt uneasy, knowing how much the Bremertons valued their privacy.

Deputy Schneider parked beside her car.

"Thanks," she said. She got out of the patrol car and glanced at the house. It was hard to believe everything that had happened. She said a silent prayer for Mr. and Mrs. B.'s safety.

"Ma'am?"

She turned to the deputy.

"I need to escort you out," he said.

"Sure, of course." As she approached her blue compact car, the echo of men's voices drifted to her from the deputy's shoulder radio. She caught part of the conversation. Someone said, "Mountain Pass Drive" and "white minivan." She guessed they were in pursuit of the vehicle Mia's kidnapper was driving.

Hope sparked in her chest. She calmly slid behind the wheel of her car. It was foolish to think she could help. However, her love for Mia drove her to want to do something.

A familiar feeling of helplessness chilled her heart. She would not accept it. Even though she'd been unable to save Greta from their horrible parents, that didn't mean she'd give up on baby Mia.

Carly pulled out of the driveway and the deputy followed her onto the main road. She should find temporary lodging somewhere, perhaps at the Juniper Inn. They knew her there since Renee, the owner, was in Carly's Bible study group.

She'd get a room later. Right now even the most comfortable room would offer little solace since Mia was out there, frightened, being held captive by a stranger. The image of Mia's red, crying face inspired Carly to follow her heart, even if it landed her in trouble.

She drove a bit, a plan forming in her head. She pulled into the Juniper Inn parking lot and Deputy Schneider drove past, lights flashing.

Waiting until he was out of sight, she left the parking lot and headed for Mountain Pass Drive. It was a long shot, but she didn't know what else to do.

Carly was desperate to save Mia.

If she happened to find the minivan, or even

show up at the scene when police found it, would they assume Carly was involved? Officially arrest her this time?

Keep your distance, reason dictated.

Help the child at any cost, her heart countered.

With firm hands gripping the steering wheel, she stayed calm and pushed aside the fear that the kidnapper might hurt little Mia. Who could possibly look at her sweet face and want to do her harm?

A few minutes later, as she approached Mountain Pass Drive, she hesitated at a four-way stop. She was about to press the accelerator when a car sailed through the intersection.

"Yikes!" Carly cried out. Through her rearview, she spotted the vehicle that sped off.

A minivan.

White.

"Unlikely." *Possible.*

Carly made a U-turn and followed the car on the off chance it was the kidnapper. Stranger things had happened. Where were the police? Maybe she was being silly, but it was worth a try.

She wasn't sure what she'd do once she caught up to the minivan. In the meantime, she decided to call the police and report its location. If the van happened to be the kidnapper's vehicle, Carly would make sure it didn't disappear, along with Mia.

She pulled out her phone to call 9-1-1.

In the distance, two police cars were blocking the road.

The minivan took a sharp right turn and went off-road, heading directly into the forest.

What was the driver thinking? There was no way out, nowhere to escape.

It had to be the kidnapper.

The minivan didn't slow down.

Neither did Carly.

She made a sharp right turn and clung to the steering wheel, her little compact bobbing up and down on the uneven terrain. This would destroy her car for sure.

She didn't care.

The minivan swerved left…

And went nose first into a ravine.

"Mia!" Carly cried.

FOUR

Carly slammed her brakes so she wouldn't go careening over the edge. She flung open the door and dashed toward the ravine. She heard men shouting behind her and didn't care. The only thing that mattered was getting to Mia, making sure she was okay.

She realized the ravine wasn't terribly steep, and the back end of the car was only about five feet down. Just then the driver's door opened. A woman with brown hair, wearing a tan raincoat and sunglasses, fought her way past the airbag and got out of the car.

"What's the matter with you?" Carly said.

The sound of Mia's cries echoed from the van, spiking adrenaline through Carly's body. The kidnapper started for the back seat.

"Don't you dare touch that little girl!" Carly dropped down to the trunk of the car with a thump.

The woman, who wore large-framed sunglasses, glanced at Carly.

Carly suddenly realized the danger of the situation. What if the kidnapper had a weapon?

Instead of reaching for a gun, the woman took off.

"Stop right there!" Carly shouted, wanting the police to arrest her and make the kidnapper answer for absconding with the little girl. But the woman had already disappeared into the woods.

Carly opened the minivan's door and smiled at Mia, who was securely strapped into a car seat.

"Shh, it's okay, baby girl."

Mia continued to wail. Was she hurt? Suffering from whiplash?

Carly sang softly to calm her down, making up her own lyrics. "Precious little baby, darling baby girl, such a sweet baby, such a sweet girl."

Awkwardly leaning against the front seat, she unbuckled Mia and pulled her into her arms. "Dear little baby, precious little girl."

Carly held Mia against her shoulder and managed to slide out of the car onto stable ground. Leaning against a nearby rock, she sang softly until the little girl stopped crying. Mia sniffled and coughed a few times, then laid her head against Carly's shoulder and stuck her thumb in her mouth.

"That's my girl. Such a brave girl." Carly cast a quick glance into the woods where the kidnapper had disappeared.

"Freeze!" a man ordered from above.

Carly couldn't catch a break today. They probably thought she was the kidnapper.

"Lemme see your hands!"

"I'm holding a baby," she called back.

"Your hands!"

Carly was not putting this child down.

Whit couldn't believe what he just saw: Carly, in her little compact car, pursuing the kidnapper across rugged terrain. He then watched the petite blonde jump out of her car and practically dive into a ravine after the van.

That had probably crashed. With his niece inside.

Whit got out of the guard's truck and jogged toward the edge of the cliff.

A sheriff's deputy put out his hand, halting Whit and Steve. "Stay back."

"I'm the child's uncle."

Whit stopped, waited impatiently for permission to approach. Just then Detective Harper raced up to them. "Where is she?"

"I'm sending up the perp," a male voice called from below. "I've got the baby."

Harper and the deputy pulled a woman up. Carly.

"Carly, Mia?" Whit said.

"She's okay." Carly smiled.

Warmth spread through Whit's chest.

The deputy grabbed Carly's wrist and started to cuff her.

"Harper," Whit said. "She put her own life at risk and went after the kidnapper."

"Not much of a risk if the kidnapper is your associate."

Carly eyed the ravine. The deputy put handcuffs on Carly, but she didn't seem to notice. She was more interested in what was happening below.

"Careful, don't hold her like that," Carly directed.

Mia's cries shot a bolt of frustration through Whit's chest.

"It's okay, baby girl," Carly said softly.

Harper crouched and grabbed a kicking, screaming Mia out of the other deputy's hands. He held her against his shoulder. Mia was having none of it. She flailed her arms, smacking Harper in the face, as she continued to sob.

Whit approached and tried soothing her with sweet words. "It's okay, Mia. You're okay now."

The baby cried louder.

"Sing to her," Carly said.

"I can't sing," Whit protested.

"Oh, come on," she said in an exasperated tone, and started singing.

Not only did the baby stop crying, but also the world seemed to tip sideways. Or maybe that was his concussion acting up.

No, it was the sound of Carly's soothing voice

that made everything shift just a little, in a good way. Even though Mia was comforted by Carly's voice, it wasn't enough. The baby wanted to be in Carly's arms, not some stranger's. Mia kicked and reached for Carly.

"Let's go," the deputy said to Carly.

"Harper, come on," Whit said.

Detective Harper handed the baby to Whit, who nodded to his slinged arm. "I need two functioning arms to hold her. Better yet, I need a nanny."

On cue, Mia screamed loud enough to shatter Harper's eardrums. He tried to mollify her, but Mia had a strong will, a lot like her father, Whit thought.

"Alright, alright. Deputy Green, uncuff her." Harper motioned to Carly. The cuffs came off and Carly reached for the child. Harper hesitated before releasing her, as if letting her know he wasn't convinced this was a good idea.

The moment Mia went into Carly's arms, the baby quieted. Carly shared a grateful expression with Whit and mouthed, "Thank you."

Whit should be thanking her.

Harper started barking orders. "We're running the plates. We need a description of the kidnapper."

"Female, medium height, brown hair, tan raincoat," Whit said. "The pediatric nurse could give a better description."

"She wore glam sunglasses," Carly added. "You know, the big movie-star kind."

"Find out where they are with the plate number," Harper ordered his deputy, essentially ignoring Carly. "And then go through the minivan."

"Yes, sir." Deputy Green went to his cruiser.

A second deputy climbed up top.

"What happened to the driver?" Harper asked.

"Didn't see her."

"She took off into the woods," Carly offered.

"Without the baby," Harper said, his tone flat. "Huh."

"I've gotta head back to the hospital," Steve, the security guard, said.

Whit extended his hand. "Thanks, man, I appreciate your help."

"My pleasure."

"I need your statement." Harper motioned for Steve to join him.

Carly paced a few feet away, rocking Mia, and Whit followed.

"How is she?" he asked.

"Pretty good, considering. Such a brave girl." Carly eyed Whit.

"Shouldn't you be in the hospital?"

"It wasn't serious."

"You passed out."

"I'm fine. My niece needs me."

"Your niece is really something." Carly brushed her lips against the top of Mia's head.

Whit still couldn't believe what he'd witnessed: Carly putting her own life in danger to save Mia.

The nanny had no way of knowing what kind of person kidnapped the baby. The perp could have been violent or been armed. The thought sparked anger in his chest.

"What were you thinking?" Whit said.

"I'm sorry?"

"Going after the kidnapper like that."

"I guess I wasn't thinking. I was driven by my love for this little girl."

He must have looked puzzled by her comment because she said, "Hasn't that ever happened to you?"

"The driver could have had a gun," he continued, not wanting to think about his inability to answer her question. "She could have killed you."

She shrugged. "If it meant saving Mia's life, then it would have been worth it."

"I don't understand."

"Well, I hope someday you will." She sighed, stroking the baby's back in a smooth, rhythmic gesture.

The adrenaline rush of the last twenty minutes was taking its toll. Exhaustion whipped through him like wind on barren desert and Whit wasn't sure how much longer he could remain standing. He needed to sit down, take a breath.

He needed to feel confident that his niece was safe.

Just then Mia made a soft squeaking sound and released a sigh too profound for such a little girl.

It was obvious she felt she was in the safest place possible—in Carly's arms.

In that moment Whit realized how much he needed Carly, not for himself, of course, but for the continued care of his niece. Especially since Whit was in no condition to care for a baby by himself.

An hour later, after statements were given to police, Carly, Mia and Whit were dropped off at the Casper Lodge, where Whit had rented a suite.

She thought for sure they'd give Mia to Whit and lock Carly up.

Whit opened the door and let Carly and Mia inside the suite, while he stepped outside to finish speaking to Detective Harper. She was grateful to him for keeping her out of jail—Harper had threatened to charge her with interfering with an investigation because she'd gone after the kidnapper's minivan—and grateful that she was still able to care for Mia.

"We should make out a list of what you need, little one," Carly said.

She pulled out a pen and notepad from the wooden desk and sat down, bouncing Mia on her lap. She jotted the essentials: diapers, wipes, formula, soft foods, even toys. Carly wished they could swing by the house and pick up some of Mia's favorites, but she knew that was out of the question since it was a crime scene.

Mia squirmed to get out of her lap, so Carly set her on the wood floor, which was shiny clean, and placed pillows around her in case of accidental "plop downs." The little girl waved her arms in frustration. She wanted to play with something.

"We seriously need some toys, don't we, baby girl?" Carly scooped Mia up and went to her purse, which she'd left on the chair by the window. She usually kept an emergency teething ring in her purse for convenience's sake. As she reached for the multicolored plastic ring, she overheard male voices through the open window.

"Here, I got your piece back from the hospital," Detective Harper said.

"Thanks."

"I'll say it again, I think having Miss Winslow near the baby is a bad idea," Detective Harper said.

"She's been the child's nanny for six months."

"Still, you don't know what you're dealing with."

"Neither do you," Whit said.

"She has a record. That's all I need to know."

Carly offered the teething toy to Mia, who waved it in the air.

"Let's say you're right, and she's somehow involved," Whit said.

Carly's heart sank.

"She's obviously developed a genuine attachment to my niece."

"Which could be dangerous," Harper said.

"Wouldn't you rather I kept her close as Mia's nanny so she doesn't disappear into the wind? Especially if you're trying to figure out how or if she's involved?"

Carly stifled a gasp of disappointment. Whit truly didn't believe her.

Of course not. He was a cop.

Carly carried Mia back to their original spot and sat down. As Mia giggled and waved the teething ring, Carly considered her options. Yeah, what options? It's not like she would abandon Mia to her uncle Whit, who didn't seem up to the task of taking care of a seven-month-old. Besides, he was essentially a stranger.

A distrustful stranger. Another manipulator?

Carly thought she'd gotten through to him earlier and had seen admiration in his eyes when he said he needed her to help with Mia. That didn't jibe with what she just heard. It sounded like he was on the detective's side, that Whit's strategy was to keep Carly close so she'd lead them to the criminals.

She was pulled into that place again, the place where no one listened to her and everyone made up their own stories about Carly.

You're a selfish little girl.

No, Mama. I'll be good!

Love. All Carly wanted was for Mom to love her.

"Ga!" Mia squeaked, bringing Carly back to

the present. Mia fell forward and Carly caught her. The little girl giggled, and Carly realized this was a new game. Fall and catch.

Like God had caught Carly when she was a teenager.

God knows what's in your heart, Carly. God knows and forgives you. He loves you.

Her aunt Vicky's words brought peace to Carly's emotional torment.

"God loves me," she whispered.

She wouldn't let her past consume her. If Whit decided not to believe her, that was his choice.

Mia waved her teething ring and flopped back down, giggling. Up and down. Two, three, four times. It reminded her of life with all its ups and downs.

Carly redirected her thoughts to positive ones. Mia was okay, more than okay. She was remarkably resilient considering everything that had happened to her today. If only Carly could be so resilient.

Mia entertained herself by smacking the teething ring on the hardwood floor.

When the suite door opened and Whit entered, Carly didn't look up. She had to steel herself against his gentle nature. He was like the rest of them, she reminded herself. He didn't believe her.

"I made a shopping list of emergency essentials for the baby," Carly said.

"Emergency?"

"Have you ever been around a famished seven-month-old?"

"Can't say that I have."

"You'll want to avoid that experience if possible. We need formula and baby food, and diapers. Pronto."

"As in right now?" Whit said.

"As in an hour ago."

There was an odd silence. She wondered if he thought this was a ploy on her part to get him to leave so she could kidnap the child. She looked up, straight into his blue eyes. "We're not going anywhere."

He cocked his head slightly, as if trying to discern her honesty. She held his gaze, her heartbeat speeding up.

He doesn't believe you. No one ever believes you.

"Okay." He turned toward the door. "I'll see if Harper can give me a ride to the house to get my car."

"Wait, are you sure you should be driving with a concussion?"

"I'll be fine."

"Then I'll see you *shortly*." She emphasized the last word to drive home the time-sensitive nature of his errand.

After he left, Carly wondered if authorities had posted a deputy outside to catch her if she attempted to flee with Mia. She had no intention of leaving the lodge, especially since at the moment she felt relatively safe.

An hour later Mia started making her hungry-whining noises and Whit hadn't returned. The hospital staff probably fed Mia formula, which didn't fill her up as much as soft foods at this stage of her development. Carly would have to get creative to prevent the baby from having a full-blown tummy tantrum.

She checked her purse for something Mia could gum, like crackers or cookies, but had nothing to offer. Carly should check the lobby for suitable snacks. Maybe they had a restaurant on-site.

She grabbed her purse. Whit and the police couldn't fault her for wanting to find food for Mia, could they?

"Let's see what we can find, sweetie." With Mia in her arms, Carly opened the door and cast a quick glance across the parking lot, a new, automatic habit since the break-in at the Bremerton estate. She spotted a police cruiser parked in the corner of the lot. Whatever. She wasn't doing anything wrong by going in search of food for the baby.

Lightly bouncing Mia in her arms, Carly continued speaking to the child to keep her engaged and distracted from her hunger pangs. "What are you in the mood for, sweet thing?"

Mia squeaked a response, and then whined louder. Time was running out.

Automatic doors opened to the lobby. The lounge area was empty with the exception of a businessman working on his laptop. She approached the front desk and a young man wearing glasses and a name badge that read Kyle looked up.

"Can I help you?" Kyle asked.

"We need snacks, and quick," Carly said lightly.

"The kitchen is only open for breakfast. Our mini-mart—" he pointed behind him to his left "—has snacks and a microwave to heat things up. Pick out what you need and I'll charge it to your room."

"Wonderful, thank you."

"My pleasure."

Carly and Mia went around the corner to the mini-mart, which was basically a shelving unit of dry foods, plus a small refrigerator and freezer stocked with things like yogurt and frozen meals. On top of the freezer she spotted a basket with fresh fruit.

"This works." She picked the ripest-looking banana and turned to the shelving unit.

Perusing other choices for Mia, Carly decided on shortbread cookies.

Mia let out a squeal of hunger.

"I hear ya, kiddo." Truth be told, Carly was a little hungry herself. She opened the package of shortbread cookies. They were long and skinny, making it easy for Mia to grip and shove in her mouth. The moment she wrapped her lips around the sugary treat, her eyes lit up.

Carly chuckled. "Good, huh?"

Mia made a humming sound and sucked on the cookie. A banana and cookie should keep her happy until Whit returned. Items in hand, Carly headed into the hall. Male voices drifted from the front desk.

"You can't or you won't give me the room number?" a man said in an angry voice.

"It's lodge policy—"

"You wanna die today, kid?"

Carly froze.

"Sir, I'm going to have to ask you to leave," the young man said.

"The last name is Whittaker. I need his room number."

Mia giggled and Carly sucked in a quick breath. Did the man hear the baby? Silence rang in her ears.

"Now!" the man shouted.

Carly sighed with relief. He hadn't heard Mia.

"I… Please don't shoot me," Kyle pleaded.

Shoot him?

Carly analyzed her best escape route. If she took off down the hall, would he hear her? Should she stay put? Hide in the mini-mart?

"I won't ask again," the man said, his voice low. "Room number and key card."

A few seconds passed. "Five thirty-seven," Kyle said.

The sound of scuffling was followed by a thump. She guessed the attacker assaulted the front desk clerk.

"I can't have you calling the police," the deep voice said.

Carly motored down the hall toward the red exit sign above the door. At least if the creep went to Whit's room she'd be at the opposite end of the complex.

Mia giggled as she bounced up and down in Carly's arms.

They were close, so close to the exit.

Just then a guest opened his door and saw Carly running. "Are you okay?"

The assailant might have heard that. She didn't turn around, couldn't bear to look.

Taking a sharp right, she spotted a housekeeping cart beside an open door in the hallway. She darted into the room and shut the door. Took a few steps away from the door.

"What are you doing?"

Carly turned to see a twentysomething housekeeper hovering beside the bed, holding a pillow in her hand. Carly put her forefinger to her lips. A few seconds passed.

She glanced around the room. It had dual access, sliding doors leading to the outside. New plan: she'd slip out and hide somewhere until help arrived.

Then she realized police weren't coming because they didn't know about the assailant.

She'd have to call them for help. Again.

"Call the police," Carly said. "Someone's after me and the baby."

The young woman's face paled as she pulled out her cell phone.

Carly started for the sliding door.

Pounding on the glass made her jump back. She snapped her gaze from the sliding door to the hallway door. She was trapped.

FIVE

Whit opened his door to an empty room.

Disappointment arced through him. Was Detective Harper right? Had she left with the baby?

"Carly?" He slid the shopping bag onto a chest of drawers.

Harper suspected Carly had her own agenda, and now she and Whit's niece were gone. Was she involved in a baby-smuggling operation? Whit didn't know, he'd never dealt with a case like this before.

"Back up," Whit said, catching himself. He tended to go to the dark side, the worst-case scenario.

Yet he'd read sincerity in Carly's eyes when she said she and the baby would be right here, waiting for him.

Maybe she put the baby down for a nap.

He went to the bedroom and froze in the doorway. A chair lay on its side and a table by the window had been overturned. It looked as if someone had lost it and took out his or her frustration on the furniture.

Or there had been a violent struggle.

Whit called Detective Harper.

"On my way," Harper answered.

"Excuse me?"

"A 9-1-1 call came in, and the deputy I left at the lodge isn't responding."

"You left a deputy here?"

"To keep an eye on Miss Winslow. Is she—"

"Gone."

"And my deputy is missing. I'll be there in five minutes."

Whit pocketed his phone. He couldn't wait five minutes, or even five seconds. His niece and the nanny were missing, potentially taken by a violent man who'd also taken out a police officer.

Whit looked for clues as to what happened to Carly and the child. There was no sign of forced entry. Had she known whoever had come to the door? Let him in before realizing her mistake? Or was it someone posing as a cop, pretending to be on her side?

He fought self-recrimination that he'd failed, that his niece would be lost forever.

Cop mode. That's how he had described his demeanor to Carly back at the river, and that had to be his mind-set right now. He needed to emotionally detach in order to find them.

As he headed toward the lobby, he scanned the

parking lot and noticed the squad car. He heard a man moaning and searched the surrounding woods, where he found a deputy on the ground, clutching his head.

Whit kneeled beside him. "Take it easy. What happened?"

"She left the room and went to the lobby with the kid. I got out to see what she was doing and was hit from behind."

"Help is on the way." Whit stood.

"Where are you going?" the deputy said.

Whit put up his hand to silence the deputy from suggesting Whit stay out of it. Whit was injured, but he was also a skilled detective and knew that when someone went missing, every minute was critical.

His niece. Missing. And it was his fault.

He approached the entrance to the lobby and pulled his arm out of the sling. If he encountered the assailant, he didn't want to seem at a disadvantage.

The main doors automatically opened. There was no one at the front desk, no one in the lobby area. Whit checked behind the counter and found a twentysomething clerk with a name badge that said Kyle unconscious on the floor. Whit felt for a pulse. Strong and steady. From the look of the goose egg on his head, the young man would have a killer headache when he regained consciousness.

"Kyle, can you hear me?" Whit said.

He didn't answer.

Suddenly a guy popped up from beneath a table in the lobby. Whit aimed his firearm. "Hands!"

"Don't shoot, don't shoot," the guy said, squinting.

"Did you make the 9-1-1 call?"

"Yes, sir."

Whit lowered his gun and flashed his badge. "Tell me what happened."

"A big guy came in demanding someone's room number and threatened to shoot the clerk."

"Where's the guy now?"

"He left."

"Was he alone?"

"I think so," the man said.

"Did you see a woman and a baby?"

"They came in first. Went to the snack shop." He pointed.

"Did the assailant go after them?"

"I'm not sure."

"Did you see him leave with the woman and child?" Whit pressed.

"The guy left out the front. I didn't see the woman leave."

Whit knew Carly was smart and extremely protective of Mia. She had fled shooters at the house, and climbed down a ravine to get to Mia. If Carly sensed trouble, she would have taken off in the opposite direction.

He popped his head into the snack area as he

passed, then continued toward the opposite end of the lodge. Pounding echoed in the distance.

Carly wouldn't relinquish the child without a fight. Was that what the banging was about? Was someone trying to beat their way into a room where Carly had taken refuge?

He turned a corner, saw the housekeeping cart in the hall and figured that Carly was hiding in one of the rooms. He knocked on a door.

No answer.

He tried another door.

It opened, and he jerked sideways as someone swung an ironing board at his head. The attacker awkwardly stumbled forward.

Carly. She spun around to take another swing.

Whit put up his hands. "Carly, it's me."

Her cheeks were flushed; her colorful eyes flared wildly. A baby's cries reminded him why Carly had gotten herself worked up into this violent state.

"The sliding door," she blurted out. "He's there."

Whit motioned her into the room. "He can't get in, and even if he does, I'm here. I'll protect you."

He hoped he could make good on that promise.

Once inside the room, he introduced himself to the housekeeper, Deanne, who handed Mia back to Carly. Whit called Harper and gave him an update, including their room number.

As he started toward the sliding door to investigate, Carly gripped his arm. "Please don't."

The genuine concern in her voice made him pause.

"Without you, Mia has no one," she said.

Right, it was Mia she was asking for, not herself.

"Be an uncle today, not a cop, okay?" she said.

The banging on the slider continued. Carly bit her lower lip. Whit placed a gentle hand on her shoulder. Truth was, he didn't want to get into a shootout in such close proximity to these women and his niece. He motioned them toward the bathroom.

"Come on, Deanne! Open the door!" a muffled voice called through the glass.

Whit eyed the housekeeper. "Were you expecting someone?"

She shook her head that she wasn't.

"Dee, please open the door. I have a surprise for you," a muffled, male voice pleaded.

"Actually, it kinda sounds like my boyfriend," Deanne said.

"Stay back," Whit ordered the women and went to the door. He peered through a crack in the curtain and spotted a twentysomething male with messy black hair and round, wire-rimmed glasses.

"Looks like Harry Potter, with black hair?" Whit said.

Deanne chuckled. "Yeah, that's him."

Whit opened the door.

"Who are you?" the kid said in an accusatory tone.

"Detective Whittaker. Get inside." Whit scanned the property, not seeing any signs of danger.

"Mark, what are you doing here?" Deanne said.

"I wanted to surprise you with these." He pulled a small bouquet of flowers from behind his back. He glanced from Whit to Carly, back to Deanne. "What's going on?"

Deanne gave her boyfriend a hug. "I'm so glad to see you."

Mark looked at Whit for an explanation.

"There's a gunman on the premises," Whit said. "Police are en route."

"Whoa," Mark said.

"How did you know where Deanne was?" Whit asked.

"We were texting, and I waited until she was cleaning her favorite room to give her flowers. It's…it's our six-month anniversary."

Deanne broke the hug and leaned back. "You are so sweet."

Whit noticed Carly look away, as if she was embarrassed to be eavesdropping on this intimate moment.

"We'll stay put until we're notified it's safe,"

Whit said to the couple as they gazed lovingly into each other's eyes.

He motioned for Carly to join him in the kitchenette.

"Why did you leave our room?" Whit asked.

"Mia was having a food meltdown and you weren't back, so I went in search of snacks."

He eyed his niece, who wore a ring of cookie crumbs around her mouth. "Sorry I took so long to get back." He brushed a crumb off Mia's cheek. "At first when I entered the room I thought…"

"That I'd left with your niece," she said.

"At first, yes."

"That doesn't surprise me. I overheard you and Detective Harper talking about keeping me close, so he could figure out who I was working with," she said in a clipped tone.

"Carly, you and I haven't known each other that long," he tried to explain.

"You obviously see how much I love this child."

"Yes." He sighed. Of that he was sure. "My goal is to protect you and Mia. I also think you may know more about my brother and sister-in-law's disappearance than you think."

"I've told you the truth about what happened," she countered.

"I'm not disputing that. Since you lived with them, a random memory might come to you that can help us piece together this case. Therefore, keeping you close both helps me care for Mia and could potentially help with the investigation into her parents' disappearance."

"Of course," she said, her voice flat.

He didn't want her to think this was all business, that he didn't have a heart. Then again, letting his emotions seep into his thought process could put them in danger.

"When I saw the trashed bedroom I thought you and Mia had been kidnapped."

"Yeah...that could have happened," Carly said. "I guess it's a good thing she was hungry, or we would have been sitting ducks in that room."

"Tell me what happened."

Whit listened to Carly explain how she'd gone in search of food and overheard someone demanding to know Whit's room number. He appreciated her ability to multitask, keeping the child content by swaying back and forth, while simultaneously offering a piece of banana and telling her story. As she described details of the threat, he puzzled over the assailant's knowing his whereabouts. The only people privy to his, Carly and Mia's location were lodge staff and the sheriff's office.

He didn't want to go there, didn't want to consider there was a shady cop in the mix, but at this point it was one potential explanation. If nothing else, the perps could be listening to the radio frequency and figured out where Whit was staying.

He wouldn't take chances with his niece's life,

so they'd pack up and move to a secure, secret location and disable location services on their phones. Detective Harper would have to agree that Whit's primary goal had to be protecting his niece and the nanny.

Muffled voices drifted to them from the other side of the door, awakening Harry from a fitful sleep. Someone entered the room. Harry kept his eyes closed. They weren't wearing blindfolds and Harry feared if he got a look at the kidnappers, his and Susan's lives were over.

Footsteps clicked against the vinyl flooring. "You may open your eyes."

"I'd rather not," Harry said.

"I'm wearing a mask."

Harry slowly looked up. A man wearing a clown mask stood over him, and another man in a similar mask stood guard at the door.

"Tell me about Brody Whittaker," the man said, obvious frustration in his voice.

Harry's big brother had come to the rescue. For the first time in his life, Harry was pleased about Whit's hero status.

"He's my half brother," Harry said.

"And?"

"He's a war hero and police detective."

"Is he married? Children?"

"No."

"Girlfriend?"

"I don't know."

"You don't know? He's your brother."

"We're not close."

"I don't believe you."

Rather than risk their hurting Susan to get answers, Harry decided to deflect with a semitruth, and in turn create sympathy with his captor.

"He abandoned me when I was a kid," Harry said.

"Well, he must care about you if he's protecting his niece with such vigor."

"He only cares about himself, and maintaining his hero status."

"So you dislike your brother?"

"Yes."

"We have that in common." The man paused. "After I retrieve the child, I will kill your brother for you. You're welcome."

Harry sucked in a quick breath. No, that's not what he—

The door slammed shut behind his kidnappers. Harry leaned back against the wall.

"We're going to die, aren't we?" Susan whispered.

"No, sweetheart. Whit will save us."

"Not if he's dead."

As they drove to their next location, Carly kept Mia occupied in the back seat until she'd fallen asleep. Carly was relieved that Detective Harper agreed to let them leave Miner to find safety in another town miles away. Whit had convinced the detective that the fewer people who knew about their location the better.

They were headed for Cold Creek Springs, a small tourist town tucked into the Rocky Mountains, the perfect spot to disappear, she thought. After everything that had happened in the past twenty-four hours, nothing would surprise her, not even a reappearance of today's gunman.

Which reminded her of the first gunman who'd come after her.

"Did they question the man you knocked out?" she asked.

"He got a lawyer."

"Was the clerk able to give a description of the man demanding your room number?"

"He did, and they put a BOLO out on him."

"And what about—"

"Hey, who's the detective here?"

"Sorry."

"It's okay, just teasing."

A few minutes later, they pulled into the parking lot of a small inn. "This place is far enough off the radar that we should be safe. I reserved a suite under a false name as an added precaution. We are Mr. and Mrs. Flannigan."

"Oh, okay." However, it wasn't okay. Pretending to be someone else made her uneasy. It reminded her too much of her parents.

"We have two adjoining rooms, one with a crib," Whit said as if he sensed her trepidation. "Tomorrow we can go into town and pick up a few things. I assume you'll need clothes."

"And more supplies for Mia."

"How much does she eat?" he said, in a light-hearted tone.

"Plenty. Did you get any cold medicine?"

"Was I supposed to?"

"I thought I put it on the list."

"Maybe they have a twenty-four-hour pharmacy in town."

He parked the SUV in the back behind the inn. As he glanced over his shoulder, he winced slightly.

"Did you pick up pain medicine at the store for yourself?" she said.

"I'm fine."

"Uh-huh, well, I'm a nursing student, so I can tell you're not fine."

"I've got some pain reliever in my glove box. You ready to check in, Mrs. Flannigan?"

"Sure."

She must have said it with an edge to her voice because he asked, "The thought of being married is that offensive, huh? Or is it being married to me that offends you?"

"I don't like pretending to be someone I'm not."

"Understandable. In this case it adds another level of protection. The perp at the hotel knew my last name so we've got to be extra careful." He exited the car and opened the back door.

Carly unbuckled Mia from her seat and got out, holding Mia against her shoulder.

Whit guided Carly up the stairs to the inn. She didn't miss the way he scanned the area, the parking lot and then the porch, nor could she ignore the slight touch of his hand against her back. It was almost as if he was positioning himself as a human shield against danger.

He tapped on the windowpane of the front door.

"You can't just walk in?" she asked.

"Not after 7:00 p.m."

As they waited for the owner to answer, Carly wondered how long she'd be embroiled in this mess and be forced to stay hidden.

"Maybe they'll have some snacks or something," he said, studying her.

He probably thought she was hungry, and in truth, she should be, but with everything that had happened today, she didn't have much of an appetite.

The front door opened and a couple in their late fifties greeted them.

"You must be Mrs. and Mrs. Flannigan," the man said.

Whit shook his hand and turned to Carly. "And this is—"

"Anna." Carly offered her middle name, trying

to stick as close to the truth as possible. The name rolled easily off her tongue. Maybe too easily.

"I'm Kurt and this is my wife, Trish," the innkeeper introduced.

"Please, come inside," Trish said with a warm smile.

She was petite, like Carly, and had gray highlights in her brown hair.

"What a sweet little girl," Trish said, nodding at Mia.

"She is sweet, and very tired," Carly said.

"We've set you up in the second-floor Evergreen suite," Kurt said. "Honey, why don't you show Anna upstairs and Mr. Flannigan and I will get their luggage."

When Whit didn't move right away, Carly nodded and said, "I'll see you upstairs."

Whit and Kurt went back outside, and Trish motioned Carly to the stairs.

"How old is she?" Trish asked.

"Seven months."

"The crib is all set up. We keep it around for when my grown children and the grandkids come to visit."

They reached the second floor and turned left. As they wandered down the hall, Carly noticed various photographs on the walls.

"The wall of fame," Trish said. "It started with our kids and grandkids, and then we added guests to the collection. They get a kick out of it when they come back to stay with us. They feel like they're a part of the family."

Carly hesitated in front of a photograph of a young couple and four children.

"My son, Dave, and his wife with their kids. They live in Wallace, Idaho, and come to visit every summer."

Even though the youngest boy made a goofy face for the camera, the family seemed so…happy. Carly looked away, wondering if God would grace her with the blessing of a happy family.

They passed by a room with a wooden Do Not Disturb plaque hanging from a piece of twine on the doorknob.

Carly was reminded they were not alone.

"Is the inn full tonight?" she asked.

"No. We have four rooms plus the suite, and only one room and your suite are occupied. The way your suite is set up, you're in a corner hallway so it's very private." They stepped into a small alcove and Carly saw two doors with a sign, Evergreen Suite.

"How long have you owned the inn?" Carly asked.

"It'll be three years next month. It's a lot of work, but I enjoy it, and we love the mountains."

Trish stuck a key in the door and opened the first room. It was large with a four-poster bed and floor-to-ceiling armoire.

"Here's the door to the adjoining bathroom."

Trish opened the door to the quaint bathroom complete with tub, which was good because Mia would need a bath at some point. "Here's the second room that you can use as the nursery."

They exited the other side of bathroom and entered a lovely bedroom positioned in the corner of the house. A floral spread stretched across the double bed, and a crib complete with a mobile was pushed up against the wall. Lace curtains trimmed the large windows.

"The view from this room is amazing during the day," Trish said.

Carly noticed a basket of snacks on the end table by a Queen Anne chair.

"I know it seems cramped with the crib," Trish said.

"No, it's perfect," Carly said.

"Are you hungry? I could warm up some chicken rice casserole."

"No, thanks. The snacks will be great."

"Just so you know, we also have one of these." Trish motioned to a baby monitor on the dresser.

The memory of the break-in swarmed Carly's thoughts. She couldn't take her eyes off the white monitor in Trish's hand.

"In case the baby is asleep, and you want to come downstairs for coffee or a snack."

"Thanks." Carly had no intention of leaving Mia's side. She gently placed her in the crib. Mia remained sound asleep.

"Our room is downstairs off the kitchen. We're usually up until midnight if you need anything. Or you can use the house phone and dial 0."

"Thank you very much."

"We hope you enjoy your stay with us," Trish said and shut the door.

Carly's gaze landed on the monitor again. Voices whispered from her memory.

I thought you'd be proud of me.

Proud? About you destroying our lives?

What are you talking about? It's a worthy project.

Loud pops.

Carly gasped. She'd been so traumatized by the events of the day she'd buried the memory of the Bremerton's argument. What had Mrs. B. done that had been so terrible?

Her phone rang, jarring her from her thoughts. She quickly answered, not wanting to wake Mia.

"Hello?" she whispered.

"Carly?" a male voice said.

She hesitated. "Yes?"

"Bring the baby back to Miner."

"Who is this?"

Silence, then, "You can't hide forever. We *will* find you."

"I'll die before I let you hurt this child."

"Then…you will die."

SIX

Whit opened the door and spotted Carly on the floor, trembling and hugging her knees.

"Thanks," he said, dismissing Kurt, who stood behind him. Whit moved his luggage and the grocery bag into the room and shut the door.

He wasted no time getting to Carly. He sat on the floor beside her and placed a comforting arm around her shoulder. "What is it?"

"A man called. He threatened to kill me unless I returned to Miner with the baby."

"Did you recognize his voice?"

She shook her head that she didn't, and then looked at him with reddened eyes. "He's coming for us, for me and the baby."

"Let's talk in the other room so we don't wake Mia."

She grabbed the baby monitor and he guided her through the bathroom to the second room.

"You're safe, Carly. We deactivated the GPS on our phones, so no one knows where we are."

She nodded and sat in a rocking chair. "He knew my number. How could he know my number?"

Whit shifted onto the edge of the bed, close enough to reach out and place a calming hand over her trembling fingers, but he didn't. She was squeezing her hands together as if she were praying, or struggling to maintain her composure, or a little of both.

"What did the caller say, exactly?" he asked.

"That I can't hide forever. That they would find me and the baby."

Whit touched her hand, hoping to ease her fears.

"I told him I'd die before I let anything happen to Mia." She paused. "And he said, 'Then you will die.'" She squeezed her hands even tighter. "Are you sure they can't find us?"

"Absolutely. No one knows we're here except for Detective Harper."

She rolled her eyes.

"He's a good cop who's frustrated because he doesn't have all the information he needs."

"You mean my background?"

"I mean a lot of things, not only your background. This is a complicated case with a lot of moving parts."

She nodded, although she seemed deep in thought.

"What is it?" Whit said.

"Before he called I remembered an argument Mr. and Mrs. B. were having before the break-in. Mr. B. accused her of destroying their lives."

"Destroying their lives how?"

"I don't know."

"But you remembered the argument, which is helpful."

"Is it?" she said, sarcasm in her voice.

"Of course. Anything you remember about Harry and Susan could help the case. For now, let's take it easy. It's been an intense day. Let's get some sleep. I can take the first Mia shift."

"That's my job."

"You've gone above and beyond your job description. You need a good night's sleep."

"No more than you." She motioned to his arm. "How's the gunshot wound? Your concussion?"

"I'll manage. I'm used to being wounded on the job."

"You're here as an uncle, Whit, not a cop. You didn't deserve to be shot any more than I deserved to be considered a suspect."

"True on both counts. Try to understand, local law enforcement must take everything into consideration."

"Like my past."

"Your past, my brother's business, whatever his wife was involved in."

"I have an idea. I have passwords to some of her email accounts if you want to—"

"Tomorrow. You need to rest. I need to rest," he muttered.

Although desperate to find his missing brother, Whit knew his primary goal had to be protecting Mia, and a good night's sleep would help him stay sharp.

Whit stood and glanced around the room. "You have everything you need?"

"Mostly, except clean clothes."

"Hang on." He quietly went back to the second bedroom and grabbed the brown bag. Returning to Carly, he pulled a Peaceful Pines Inn sweatshirt and Rocky Mountains sweatpants out of the bag. "That's all they had downstairs in the gift corner. We'll go shopping tomorrow."

"Thanks."

He hesitated by the door. "If you're still upset about the call, I'll sit in that chair until you fall asleep."

"No, it's okay. I'll be fine. I'll relieve you in a few hours."

"Or you could get a full night's sleep. That wouldn't be the worst idea in the world."

She frowned, an odd expression on such an adorable face.

"What is it?" he said.

She glanced up.

"You got this look on your face," he said. "Did you remember something else?"

"I'm just tired," she said.

But he suspected there was more to it.

"Okay, then, good night."

"Good night."

The next morning Carly blinked her eyes open and took a few seconds to recall where she was and how she'd ended up here. A familiar pit settled in her stomach.

Yet she wasn't the juvenile offender waiting for Mom and Dad to visit her in lockup. She was a loving nanny and nursing student.

Who was on the run from kidnappers who had threatened her life.

She sat up in the Queen Anne chair and realized a blanket had been tucked around her. Hmm, she didn't remember bringing a blanket with her from the other room last night.

Last night. She'd lain awake after Whit shut the door, wondering if his concern about her welfare was genuine or if it was a manipulation to keep her away from the baby. Did Whit fear that when everyone was asleep and the house was quiet, Carly would make her escape and kidnap the child?

After tossing and turning for an hour, she'd given up on sleep and went into Mia's room, intending to relieve Whit of his child care duties. There was something about being close to Mia that made Carly feel grounded, at peace. Talk about the Mama Bear instinct.

She'd found Whit asleep on the bed, looking utterly content, and she didn't want to disturb him. Carly made herself comfortable in the thick-cushioned chair and prayed, because prayer always calmed her worry. It also helped her relax, so it made sense she'd drifted off to sleep.

Carly tossed the blanket aside and eyed the crib. Little Mia was asleep, sucking contently on her thumb. Her diaper must be drenched by now. She stood over the crib and realized the little girl was dressed in fresh clothes. Carly touched Mia's pants. The diaper was light, not heavy. Had Whit changed her diaper and her clothes, and fed her breakfast? Carly pressed the back of her fingers against Mia's cheek. It was warm. She must still be fighting that cold.

Carly looked at the nightstand clock radio. It read 9:07 a.m.

"Whoa, what a slacker." She went into the bathroom and spotted a note from Whit on the mirror: *Come downstairs for breakfast. I have the monitor.*

After washing her face and brushing her teeth using toiletries supplied by the inn, she put on the sweatshirt and pants and headed downstairs. Voices echoed from the dining room.

"The Rockwood Creek area is delightful this time of year," Trish said.

"Delightful? Come on, Trish," her husband, Kurt, teased.

"What's wrong with delightful?"

"The last time we went, you got stuck in a mound of snow."

"That's because it was winter, dear husband. It's lovely this time of year. No danger of mis-stepping."

"She got swallowed by a mound of snow five feet deep and she's barely five-two," Kurt said. "All I could see were purple gloves waving at me."

"Don't embarrass me," Trish said.

Carly turned the corner to the dining room. Whit was sitting at the table with Trish and Kurt, the baby monitor in front of his plate of half-eaten eggs.

"Good morning," Carly said.

"Good morning," Trish greeted.

Whit stood and pulled out a chair for her. "Sleep good?"

"Yes, thanks." She sat down and he pushed in her chair.

"Did you change and feed the baby?"

"I did," he glanced at Trish. "Although I had help. I brought Mia downstairs for a bit so she wouldn't wake you."

"Sorry I slept so late."

"No need to apologize," Trish said.

"That's what vacations are for," Kurt said. "To

sleep late and eat good food. Well, not good-for-you food, but, well, you know what I mean."

A vacation? If only this was a vacation, Carly thought.

Another guest entered the dining room from the salon.

"Anna, this is Roger Burns," Trish said. "He's here with his wife, Ingrid, on a second honeymoon."

Carly nodded to the tall, blond man in his forties with a slight beard.

"Good morning," Roger said, refilling his mug of coffee from the pot on the table. "That's a cute little girl you've got, Mrs. Flannigan."

"Anna," she said, not feeling quite so bad if he used her real middle name. "Thank you." Carly forced a pleasant smile. This stranger had seen Mia? That meant another person could identify them, knew where they were hiding out.

Whit's gentle hand touched her shoulder. The connection stopped her panic from spinning out of control. He must have sensed the direction of her thoughts.

"I was going to pick up a few things in town," he said.

"The baby and I will come with you."

Whit nodded and she thought she saw a slight smile crinkle his eyes. She found herself hesitating before looking away, enjoying the moment a little too much. He was not her friend, nor could he ever be. They had the same goal—keep Mia safe—yet at the end of the day he was a cop and she had a record. Once this case was solved, he'd disappear from her life.

Whit grabbed a basket on the table. "How about some muffins or fruit?"

"That would be great."

He placed the basket in front of her and reached for a plate of melons and strawberries.

"I can scramble some eggs if you'd like," Trish offered.

"Fruit and muffins are fine," Carly said.

"I'll get some fresh coffee going." Kurt grabbed the pot. "Can I get you anything else while I'm up, Anna?"

"I'll have a cup of coffee whenever."

"About five minutes."

"Thanks." For a brief second she felt normal, a part of a family, as she sat at the table making pleasant conversation.

"Nice meeting you," Roger said, and went back into the salon with his book.

That shook her out of her daydream. She somewhat trusted Whit because they had a shared goal, and Carly wanted to trust the owners of the inn, but Roger and his wife were strangers.

Carly noticed a newspaper on the table. She was tempted to ask if there'd been any coverage about the Bremerton break-in, and chose not to since Roger could still be within earshot.

Whit must have read her thoughts. "News was pretty boring today," he said.

"How's the arm?" she asked.

"Okay."

She suspected it pained him. "You still have the sling?"

"Upstairs."

"Good."

His phone vibrated with a text and his brows furrowed.

"Everything okay?" she asked.

"I'd better take this." He looked at her. "Unless you want me to…"

"I'm fine. Go ahead. I'll be up in a few minutes."

Whit took the baby monitor and headed for the stairs.

"Sling that arm," she called after him.

"Will do," he answered.

Carly reached for the butter dish.

"He's so attentive," Trish said. "You've got yourself a good one."

Carly nodded and felt a smile crease her lips. This time it wasn't forced. Trish was right. Whit seemed like a genuinely good guy.

"I helped him with the baby this morning," Trish said. "You know men, they tend to be awkward with babies until they're walking and talking and playing Little League baseball."

"Yeah," Carly said.

Although Harry Bremerton had always been interested in Mia's day, what new toys she was playing with and words she'd attempted to speak. Mia's dad was nurturing and kind, much like his brother.

She had to stop admiring Whit's good qualities or else she'd be lured into a false sense of security. There was no safe place, not when it came to Carly and relationships.

"What did you have planned while you're here?" Trish said.

"Um…relaxing I guess." Although in truth she felt guilty that she wasn't studying for her NCLEX nursing exam. Staying one step ahead of the kidnappers had to take priority. "Maybe we'll do some easy hikes if the baby feels better."

"Is she sick?"

"Just the sniffles."

"There are a few wonderful spots north of town," Trish started. "I'll make you a list."

"Perfect, thanks." Carly forked melon onto her plate and selected a muffin with chocolate chips out of the basket. She took a deep breath, interlaced her fingers and said a silent prayer of thanks.

No meal should be taken for granted.

"Amen," she said softly and cut open her muffin.

"I'd better get started on the breakfast dishes before my boss threatens to dock my pay," Trish said.

"I heard that," Kurt responded from the kitchen.

They were an adorable couple, a man and woman who showed love through humor and kindness.

Carly enjoyed the peace and quiet for a few minutes until anxiety whispered in her mind. She wasn't sure why. Maybe because Whit hadn't returned, or because she worried that Mia had awakened and he needed help taking care of her. After all, the child hadn't even met her uncle until yesterday and if she awoke suddenly to him standing over her crib...

A flash of memory rushed to the surface, being frightened in lockup, a man standing on the other side of the bars, watching her.

"Here's the coffee," Kurt said.

Carly jumped at the sound of his voice.

"Or maybe you should skip the coffee today," he teased.

"Sorry, I was thinking about something else."

"Thinking. Always gets me in trouble." He placed a full pot on the table. "You need cream and sugar?"

"No, I'm good."

Kurt went back into the kitchen, leaving her alone. She promised herself not to go to the dark place. She thought she'd put the past behind her, worked through the fear of not feeling safe. This new threat must have triggered buried memories. Of course it did. Here she was again, trying to protect a child, like she'd tried to protect Greta from her manipulative parents.

She couldn't help Greta.

Nothing would stop her from protecting Mia.

Carly finished her breakfast and took her mug of coffee upstairs. As she reached the second floor, a tall, sophisticated-looking woman sauntered toward her. Carly was about to offer a greeting, but the woman studied her phone as if she didn't welcome interaction. Carly respected her privacy and continued to the suite she and Whit were sharing with Mia.

She went directly to the crib, checking Mia's cheeks. Still warm. They'd have to get a baby thermometer and acetaminophen first thing. The low tone of Whit's voice drifted from the other bedroom through the bathroom. Carly couldn't hear what he was saying, but he sounded intense.

She went into the bathroom, found a cloth in the cabinet and rinsed it under cool water. Just as she squeezed it out, Whit stepped into the doorway.

"We need to talk," he said softly so as not to disturb Mia.

She followed him into the other room and he shut the door. "Were you being honest when you said my brother knew about your criminal history?"

Defense mechanisms clicked into place. "Yes."

"Even the part about you being forbidden from seeing your little sister?"

He might as well have slugged her in the gut. She couldn't speak at first.

"Carly?"

"Mr. Bremerton knew," she said, stoic. She could feel herself shutting down, putting distance between herself and this man she thought might have given her the benefit of the doubt.

"Then explain to me why he hired you," he said.

"You'd have to ask him," she shot back.

"Come on, help me out here."

"Who told you about Greta?"

"Does it matter? Look, my priority is Mia's welfare."

"A child you didn't even know until yesterday." She was on the offense, wanting to hurt Whit before he could hurt her.

"Look, if you were a danger to your own sister, how can I, in good conscience, keep you around my niece?"

Her heart sank. He'd been the one person in this whole mess with the potential to believe in her, to have faith that there was more to her story, and now he was turning his back on Carly, too, just like her parents and authorities.

Maybe she should have kept fighting, Aunt Vicky had said softly to their minister. She didn't know Carly was nearby, and she'd never say the words directly to Carly because she knew it would upset her niece. It made Carly wonder if she had found a better lawyer and kept explaining her situation until someone actually listened, would she have been vindicated instead of vilified?

"I mean if your own parents took out a restraining order—"

"Stop," Carly interrupted Whit. "You know nothing about my childhood, or my criminal parents. They used their children to help perpetrate their crimes. My parents…" Her voice cracked. She cleared her throat. She had to say this, had to finally defend herself. "My parents manipulated me with the promise of love, when all they had to offer was emotional abuse. Mother wanted to keep me away from Greta because I was trying to protect her. I could expose my parents if I talked to cops, which I wouldn't because I'd been brainwashed into believing cops would destroy my life. And, in the end, they did."

"Carly—"

"I have lived with the oppressive brand of being a bad seed, a juvenile delinquent. Do you have any idea what that does to a person? To a child who was only trying to do the right thing out of love for her sister?"

He clenched his jaw and didn't respond. Good, because she had more to say.

"I've been taking care of Mia for six months and she has flourished under my care," she continued. "Your brother hired me despite my background because he believed in giving me another chance. He checked my references and was satisfied. I told him what had happened to me as a kid, and he was still satisfied. I didn't have to, by the way. My juvenile record was expunged, so technically it never happened. My background didn't bother your brother. I'll go out on a limb here and guess he could relate, that he knew what it was like to need another chance, maybe even from his own family because he never mentioned you or your parents, or anyone else he was related to. Not once. So, before you cast aspersions on my dysfunctional mess of a family, you'd better be willing to take a hard look at your own. Now, if we're done, Mia has a fever and I'm going to go cool her down with a damp washcloth."

Not waiting for a response, she turned and went into Mia's room.

Whit stood there, trying to process Carly's diatribe.

Manipulative and emotionally abusive parents? Criminals? How had that information not popped up before now?

He pulled out his phone to call his tech person in Dallas. Hesitated. Glanced through the bathroom. A part of him wanted to take Carly at her word, believe everything she'd said. The detective part of him needed confirmation, so he made the call.

"How's it going, Detective Whittaker?" Megan the tech answered.

"It's been better."

"Bored, huh?"

"Not exactly. I need a favor, a personal favor."

"Go for it."

"I need information on Carly Winslow, alias Garber. Late twenties, from Denver. Younger sister Greta."

"Dating material?" Megan teased.

"Very funny. No, a person of interest. Carly has a juvenile record, expunged, which might help you track her down. Text me when you find something?"

"Of course. Stay out of trouble."

"No promises." He pocketed his phone. Whit needed to clear this up and decide if Carly was friend or enemy. Straddling the fence about whether to believe her or not was an uncomfortable place to be.

He hadn't been on the fence twenty minutes ago. As he had sat at the dining table with her, he felt a strong, authentic connection. He reminded himself that was probably their dire situation coupled with his concussion that was messing with his judgment. Whit didn't trust easily, nor did he open himself up to people too quickly, so why did he find himself wanting to trust Carly?

Because of the way she'd protected Mia. That wasn't playacting. Carly was genuinely devoted to the child and right now the little girl needed that. She needed someone who loved her.

Love. He'd seen it Carly's eyes when she held the baby, sang to her.

He couldn't let that love distract him or cloud his objectivity. Whit needed to keep the protective walls up so he could see clearly, because the adorable blonde in the next room had a way of blowing his focus right out of the water, either with her effusive and seemingly innocent charm, or her defensive accusations.

So, before you cast aspersions on my dysfunctional mess of a family, you'd better be willing to take a hard look at your own.

She wasn't wrong. Whit and Harry's family had its own share of kinks and complications. Somehow, she'd homed in on that as well, on the fact that Harry had gotten himself into mischief as a teenager and needed his share of forgiveness from Whit's mom and stepfather. Whit wasn't around much during those years since he was committed to his law enforcement career, but he'd heard plenty from Mom, who'd asked Whit to come home and have a heart-to-heart with his little brother.

By the time Whit got a decent vacation and was able to get home, it was pretty clear that Harry had completely written off his older brother. The anger, the resentment brimming in Harry's eyes, was obvious, and Whit knew why: because he'd failed him so miserably.

Harry's accident when he was ten had been

Whit's fault, and seven years had been too long for Harry to wait for an apology, an explanation about why his older brother didn't take better care of him.

Eyes brimming with angry tears, Harry had clenched his jaw tight, listened to Whit's lecture on making better choices and didn't utter a word. When Whit was done, Harry left the room and didn't return home for three days, staying at a friend's house until Whit left town. Harry's anger had been justified at ten years old. By seventeen he should have gotten past it, not let it eat away at him and cause him to misbehave.

Really, Whit? Have you gotten over feeling ashamed about the incident? No, he hadn't. He spent the last twenty years committing himself to the military and law enforcement, probably hoping on some level that he'd bury the shame once and for all.

Look at me, Brody! I can fly!

Whit shook off the memory. Carly was right, Whit's family wasn't good at giving second chances or offering forgiveness. Which was another reason he'd decided to join the army at eighteen.

He needed to redeem himself.

"Why am I thinking about this?"

Because Carly had challenged him, she'd hit too close to home, especially considering she was a stranger.

A stranger who knew Whit's brother better than Whit did. Ostracizing her was a bad idea. She held the key to his niece's comfort and happiness, and maybe even had answers that could help them find Harry.

Whit should apologize to Carly, at least for his tone. She had to understand his motivation: he was driven by his love for his niece and the need to protect her.

He stepped into the makeshift nursery. "Carly?"

She glanced over her shoulder, swiping at her eyes. His gut twisted. He did that, upset her to the point of tears.

"I'm sorry if I offended you," he said.

"Whatever."

"You have to understand where I'm coming from."

"Sure, I understand. I'm used to it."

"Cut me a little slack. Just when I start to trust you, something else pops up like the restraining order."

"Not every answer is a simple one. A person's past can be very, very complicated. I thought for sure you would understand that."

A few seconds of silence stretched between them. "I'm very conflicted," he confessed. "You obviously care deeply for Mia and have taken good care of her, but you have a record."

Carly continued to brush the cool cloth across

his niece's cheeks and down her arms. She lifted Mia's shirt to reveal a rash on her tummy.

"Fire me later," she said. "We need to get her to a doctor."

Mia whimpered, and a knot twisted in Whit's gut. That sound, the sound of a child in pain, played havoc with his soul.

"I'll find a local clinic," he said.

Carly nodded and began to sing softly to the little girl.

"It'll be okay," he automatically said, wondering if he was saying the words more for himself than for Carly.

"How long has she had a fever?" Dr. Rutherford asked.

"On and off for a few days," Carly answered, watching him check Mia's eyes, ears and nose.

"And the rash?"

"Just started," Carly said.

Thankfully Dr. Ken Rutherford, a local family practice doctor, was able to work them into his schedule. The nurse had led Carly, the baby and Whit directly into a room so Mia wouldn't expose anyone else to whatever she was fighting.

It had been an awkward hour waiting for the doctor. Whit would try to engage Carly in conversation to which Carly would offer quick, one-syllable answers. She wasn't in the mood for conversation, not only because she was worried about Mia, but also because she had constructed a wall between herself and Whit.

To think that after everything they'd been through, Whit had used a sharp, accusatory tone when questioning her about her past. She thought he had come around to believing in Carly, a little bit anyway.

She'd been so wrong.

"Appetite?" Dr. Rutherford asked.

"Still okay," Carly answered.

"Actually, she didn't eat much this morning for me," Whit offered.

Carly snapped her gaze to him. "You didn't tell me that."

Whit studied Mia.

Carly answered a few more questions from the doctor, and he handed Mia back to Carly.

"When was the last time she had acetaminophen?" the doctor said.

"Yesterday."

Dr. Rutherford looked at her questioningly, and shame flooded her cheeks.

"It's my fault," Whit said. "I was supposed to pick some up and forgot."

"I'll have the nurse give you some to hold you over until you can stop by the pharmacy," the doctor said. "If the fever persists, keep her on acetaminophen every four to six hours. I suspect it will break with the worsening of the rash."

"What's causing the rash?" Carly asked.

"Mia has roseola."

"Is that serious?" Whit said.

"No, not serious," the doctor said. "It starts with a fever and ends with a rash."

"Does she need special medication?" Whit said.

"It's a virus that will run its course. I suspect the rash will clear in a few days and this little cutie pie will be back to normal." He squeezed her foot playfully. "If not, give us a call." The doctor left the room.

Carly sat Mia down on the examining table to put on her jacket. "Why didn't you tell me she didn't eat much this morning?" she said, not looking at Whit.

"I thought… I don't know, that it was my fault."

"Your fault?"

"That I was doing something wrong when I was feeding her."

"Doubtful. Babies instinctively know what they need, and they aren't shy about asking for it. If only adults were allowed to be so direct."

She turned to Whit, holding the baby in her arms.

"If you were allowed to be direct, what would you say to me right now?" he asked.

She heard the challenge in his voice, yet wasn't sure where he was going with this line of questioning. "I'd say I'm grateful that Mia only has roseola and nothing more serious."

"And…?"

He was pushing her. Why?

"We should figure out what Mrs. B. was into, so we can help police solve this mess and get back to our lives," Carly snapped.

"And…?"

"What do you want from me?"

"The truth."

"Here we go again. You know, some of us have moved on with our lives and would like to keep our past where it belongs—in the past."

"I'm not talking about your past," he said.

"Well, I have no idea what you're talking about."

"You're upset with me."

"No kidding."

"Whatever happened to you as a kid, I'm sorry. Please try to see it from my perspective. If you were Mia's aunt and you walked into this situation, wouldn't you be just as protective and cautious as I'm being?"

He was right, and she didn't like it. She didn't like it because that would start to dissolve the walls she'd constructed around her heart.

"Let's go." She opened the examining room door.

A woman's shriek echoed down the hall.

SEVEN

Whit stepped in front of Carly and shifted her and the baby behind him. "Stay back."

"You're not going out there," she said.

It was a statement, not a question.

"You'll be safe in the room," he said.

"No, Whit. Don't leave your niece."

"She's in good hands."

"An hour ago you were questioning my integrity."

"Let's have this argument later. Call 9-1-1." He looked at her. "Now." He left the room and sneaked down the hall.

"It's a simple question. Have you seen her?" a man shouted.

"No, I haven't," a woman said.

"If you're lying to me—"

"She's not lying," Dr. Rutherford said.

"I don't believe you."

"That is your prerogative."

The doc had guts, Whit thought.

"My prerogative?"

Another scream and gasps echoed down the hall. Whit wanted to avoid a shootout in the waiting room.

He turned the corner. A short stocky guy with black hair in his midforties had the doctor in a choke hold. The guy could easily snap the doc's neck.

"He can't answer if he can't breathe," Whit said.

The guy looked at Whit. "Another smart guy, huh?"

"Nope, just a patient." He motioned to his arm in the sling.

The doc was digging his fingers into the guy's arm, trying to get air.

"If you want him to talk, you're gonna have to let go," Whit said.

A few seconds passed. Whit hoped the perp didn't snap the doc's neck in front of his patients. Trauma like that would never leave them.

Stocky Guy released the doctor and shoved him into the front desk. Rutherford collapsed on the floor, gasping for air.

"This kid, have you seen her?" He flashed a picture of Mia on his phone.

"Who is she?" Whit studied the image, pretending not to recognize his niece.

"It's not important."

"Must be if you're committing assault."

"Anyone seen her?" The guy flashed the image to the half a dozen patients in the waiting area.

Whit didn't want to put these innocents at risk. If he drew his firearm, the perp could use one of them as a shield.

"No?" the guy said to each patient. "Then I'll check for myself." The perp yanked the doctor to his feet.

Pulled a gun from his shoulder holster.

He approached Whit, who blocked the doorway to the hall.

"Come on, man, this isn't cool," Whit said.

The guy pointed the gun at the doc's head. "How about dead? Is dead cool?"

There was no way Whit would let the guy get anywhere near Carly and Mia's room and he didn't want the doc to be killed either.

"Take me," Whit said. "People need the doc. Me, not so much."

The guy considered his proposal and shoved the doctor away. He motioned for Whit to lead the way. As they approached examining room one, the muffled sound of a baby crying echoed down the hall.

"Let's start down there," the guy said.

Whit instinctively slowed down, and the guy pressed the gun into his back. "Is there a problem?"

"No problem."

Big problem. They were only fifteen or so feet from Carly and Mia.

He had to end this before they opened the door to Carly's examining room.

Whit took a deep breath. He was the last line of defense for Carly and the baby. He didn't want a repeat of yesterday.

Of being overpowered by a gunman.

Ten feet away.

He slowed his breathing and tried to get a handle on the adrenaline pumping through him. The guy probably didn't think Whit, with one arm in a sling, was a threat. He silently thanked Carly for ordering him to re-sling his arm.

Five feet away.

He prepared himself for an assault. Fisted his hand.

A door cracked open behind them, distracting the gunman.

Whit elbowed the guy in the ribs and dodged out of the line of fire. The examining room door slammed shut. Whit shoved the guy back against the wall with such force the weapon jarred loose from his hand and hit the floor. Whit kicked it into an open room. The guy slammed his fist against Whit's shoulder injury and he reeled back.

The guy made a move for his gun.

Whit withdrew his firearm and yanked his other arm out of the sling. "Police, freeze!"

The guy turned and slowly raised his hands.

"Hands against the wall," Whit ordered.

The corner of the gunman's eye twitched slightly. "You're a cop. Just my luck."

"I said, hands against the wall."

Sirens echoed in the distance, and the perp cocked his head, eyes flaring.

The guy turned slowly to face the wall. Whit didn't have cuffs, so they'd just have to wait.

Another examining room door suddenly opened.

The guy grabbed the patient, a woman in her forties.

She screamed and he wrapped his arm around her, using her as a shield. There was no way Whit could fire his weapon and the guy knew it.

With a victorious smile, the perp backed up and then shoved the woman at Whit, who braced her fall. The guy took off through the waiting area.

"Are you okay?" he asked the woman.

She nodded that she was. Whit went in pursuit, fearing that even without his gun the guy would take an innocent patient hostage.

Instead, he sped out the front exit. Whit paused in the waiting area to ask everyone if they were okay. They nodded that they were.

Whit bolted outside and caught sight of the guy peeling out of the lot in an SUV. Whit went back into the clinic, wrote down the plate number on a piece of paper and gave it to the receptionist, who was cowering beside the desk.

"It's okay. He's gone," Whit said. "Give this to police when they arrive."

He handed the young woman the slip of paper and went to check on Carly and the baby, realizing how badly things could have gone, how close they'd come to disaster.

It's okay. Carly and the baby were safe.

He opened the door to their examining room. Empty.

A familiar feeling curdled his gut, the same feeling he'd experienced this morning at the lodge.

"Carly?" He noticed the open window and crossed the room to look outside. He saw his truck still parked out back, not that she could have taken it without the keys.

Man, you either trust her or don't trust her.

Although his intellect fought it, he realized he trusted her with Mia's life, which made him wonder...

"Carly!" he shouted out the window.

She popped out from behind a gray sedan in the parking lot.

"What are you doing out there?" he said.

"Hiding."

"Come back inside." He motioned to her.

She glanced nervously from side to side before crossing the parking lot. He took a fussy Mia from Carly's arms and wanted to offer his other hand to help Carly back inside but needed both arms to keep Mia secure against his chest.

Carly didn't seem to need his help. She deftly climbed through the window.

"You have to stop doing that," he said.

"What?" She reached for Mia.

"Disappearing."

"I'm used to watching out for myself and I had to protect the baby."

"That's *my* responsibility."

"Well, if something happens to you—"

"You mean like yesterday."

"No, I meant—"

"We've gotta go." He motioned her out of the room.

"What happened in the waiting area?"

"I'll tell you in the truck."

"How did they find us?"

"No idea." He led her down the hall to a side door and into the parking lot, continuing to scan the area for trouble. He wouldn't assume they were out of danger and wanted to get back to the inn, where they'd be safe. Maybe. Hopefully.

"Wait!" a man called from the clinic.

Whit encouraged Carly to walk faster. He pressed the fob, unlocked the door and handed her the keys. "Wait in the truck."

She did as ordered without any discussion. Slipping his hand inside his jacket for his gun, he turned…

A sheriff's deputy was heading toward him.

Whit dropped his hand to his side to keep it in plain sight.

"You're the guy who chased off the assailant?"

"Yes, sir." Whit pulled out his ID and badge. "Brody Whittaker. Dallas PD."

The deputy, whose name tag read Logan, was in his midtwenties with a crew cut.

"I'll need your statement."

"I understand. Right now it's critical that I get my niece and my friend back to our bed-and-breakfast. They're in danger and we're not sure who's after them. This started back in Miner. Contact Detective Harper with the Summit County Sheriff's Office for confirmation."

"Did your friend witness what happened today?"

"No, sir."

"Then I'll have a deputy take them back to your inn."

"Sorry, can't do that. I'm responsible for their well-being," Whit said. "You can send a deputy to the inn for my statement or I'll give you a brief statement now. I'd rather not spend any more time here than necessary."

"Where are you staying?" Deputy Logan asked.

"Peaceful Pines Inn, under the name Flannigan to keep our whereabouts confidential."

"Hang on." The deputy took a few steps away and made a call, probably to his supervisor.

As minutes ticked by, Whit grew more irritated

as he scanned the premises. Talk about being exposed. Then again the assailant most likely got as far away as possible in order to avoid authorities, plus the attacker didn't know that Whit was Mia's uncle. He could have assumed Whit was a random cop at the right place at the right time.

The sound of a crying little girl echoed from inside the SUV. Whit glanced at the car. Even though the windows were tinted and he couldn't see Carly, he offered a slight smile to ease her fears. She must still be flooded with adrenaline.

Deputy Logan turned to Whit. "Kurt confirmed a Mr. and Mrs. Flannigan and their daughter are staying at the inn." He handed Whit's wallet back. "I'll stop by later to get a full statement."

"Sounds good."

Deputy Logan went back into the clinic. Whit jogged to the SUV and opened the door.

"What happened?" Carly asked as she held the baby, trying to comfort her.

"It's all good," Whit said. At least, until the next attack.

On the drive back to the inn, Carly noticed Whit constantly checking the rearview and side-view mirrors. He'd even passed by the inn's driveway a few times to determine if they were being followed. Once he was confident they weren't, he turned onto the long drive.

Ever since they left the clinic, he'd occasionally ask how she was doing. Was she anxious? Nervous? Scared?

Although still frustrated and upset, she was no longer in fight-or-flight mode. She guessed that's what he was trying to determine.

Now, safely in their room, Carly played with Mia on the floor while Whit puzzled through what happened at the doctor's office.

"It's like they're following us but don't know our exact location," Whit said.

"Did he ask for Mia by name?"

"No, he asked if anyone had seen her and flashed a picture on his phone. Which makes me think he was canvassing the area because he didn't know her specific location."

"That's a relief."

"Why check a doctor's office?" He turned to Carly. "Who knew she was sick?"

"Her parents and the cook because she was making special food for Mia." Carly sighed. "I'm glad she wasn't there when the men broke in."

"The cook?"

"Mrs. Bright. She comes to the house three times a week to prepare meals for the family. She purees organic fruits and vegetables for Mia."

"She wasn't there yesterday?"

"No, she switched her days because she had a family conflict."

Whit nodded, not looking satisfied with her answer or anything for that matter. He readjusted items on a small desk in the corner, looked outside and then straightened books on the shelf across the room. Carly felt his frustration.

"I think checking Mrs. Bremerton's email could help," Carly said.

Whit shook his head.

"You don't think it will help?" she said.

"I'm a cop, Carly. I go by the book, not break into people's emails."

"We're not breaking in. She gave me her password so I could sign on and make appointments and check things for her."

"I thought you were just the nanny?"

Carly raised her eyebrow.

"That didn't come out right. I meant they didn't hire you to be an assistant. Your job was—is—to take care of Mia, not do other stuff like, I don't know... Now I'm rambling because I've offended you. I'm sorry." He paused. "I'm sorry about before, too."

His apology seemed genuine and her walls weakened just a little. She decided to change the subject.

"How's your bullet wound? Do I need to check the dressing?"

"Let's concentrate on this first."

"Okay, well, I think Mrs. B. would be fine with us going through her email if she thought it could help us protect Mia, don't you?" When Whit hesitated again, she grabbed his tablet off the bed.

"How about I sign in, just like I always do, and then you're not doing anything off the book?"

"Interesting expression."

Carly leaned against the bed beside Mia and signed on. Whit joined them on the floor, reaching out to steady Mia as she enthusiastically swung her arm to tap a toy xylophone the innkeepers had loaned them.

"You wouldn't know she's fighting a fever," Whit said.

"Acetaminophen does wonders." Scanning through emails, Carly said, "What am I looking for exactly?"

Whit leaned closer and she suddenly felt self-conscious. Carly hadn't showered since yesterday and although she'd washed up, she didn't have her things, including makeup.

Makeup? What are you thinking about, Carly? This man has no interest in you as a romantic prospect and has made it clear he still doesn't trust you.

"Sorry, am I crowding you?" He leaned back.

"No, I was worried that I stink since I didn't get my shower this morning."

"You're fine," he said.

Her heart jumped. Oh, boy, she'd better get a grip because this was not a relationship that had any future beyond keeping Mia safe. Only a few hours ago he'd accused her of not being the right caretaker for Mia because of Carly's past. After her rant about her parents, she thought she'd felt a shift, that Whit might be giving her another chance to prove herself, even though he knew about the restraining order meant to keep her away from her little sister.

Greta. The trauma of never seeing her again and not knowing where she ended up haunted Carly still. Even when Aunt Vicky encouraged Carly as an adult to find Greta, Carly couldn't bring herself to work past the shame of not protecting her sister from their manipulative parents.

"Did you find something?" Whit said, interrupting Carly's thoughts.

She snapped her attention to his blue eyes studying her intently.

"Sorry, not yet." She ripped her gaze from his and refocused on the tablet.

"What are all those emails from the Lancaster Society?" Whit asked.

"It's a nonprofit that raises money for children who need medical treatment. She's on the board. She volunteers for Bountiful Bravery as well, which is a church group that sponsors refugees."

"My brother goes to church?"

"Sure, we all went every Sunday. Why, don't you go to church?"

"No time for God," he said, his eyes intent on the tablet.

"You don't have to attend church on Sundays to make time for God. Watch." She closed her eyes.

"Lord, please protect us, love us and guide us through this turbulent time. Amen." She opened her eyes. "See? It's that easy."

He pointed to the tablet. "What's this one?"

Well, okay, Carly supposed God wasn't everyone's cup of tea, although she couldn't imagine life without the Lord.

Glancing back at the emails, she saw the one he was referring to with the subject line "Invest in Children: Serenity Resort." She clicked it open. "It's a reply to a donor request letter sent by Mrs. B. This person has committed to pledging twenty thousand dollars to the resort. Wow, that's a lot of money."

"Scroll down. I want to read the actual donor letter."

They both read the email inviting the recipient to invest in a property in Madagascar that was guaranteed to triple their investment in two years, boost tourism and provide an added bonus: a percentage of the profits went to fighting poverty for children.

"She sent a lot of these emails three months ago," Carly said. "Sounds like a worthy cause."

"If it's legit."

"What do you mean?"

"There are no guarantees when it comes to investing, and the email doesn't state specifically how they're going to fight poverty. Then there's

my brother's comment, the one where he accused
Susan of ruining their lives."

"What do you think that meant?"

"Maybe this fund-raiser was crossing some
legal lines and that's what Harry was referring to."

"How could raising money to build a resort ruin
their lives? Especially if it helps kids?"

"It raises questions in my mind. Madagascar is
a third-world country, Carly. People don't necessarily find it relaxing to confront poverty while
on vacation."

"True."

"It's a nice sales pitch. Anyone with extra
money would jump at the chance to triple an investment. Plus, the whole helping-kids thing eases
guilt that the investor has about making a profit
in a poverty-stricken country. I'll share this information with Harper."

Someone knocked on the door. When Whit got
up, she noticed him wince. The man needed a
break so his body could heal.

He eyed the peephole and cracked the door
open.

"A deputy is downstairs. He wants to take your
statement," Kurt said.

"I'll be right there." Whit shut the door and
turned to Carly. "You'll be okay?"

"Of course." Mia rubbed at her eyes with fisted
hands. "Someone's working herself up to a nap."

"This shouldn't take long."

Carly pulled Mia into a hug and the baby kicked her feet.

"Carly?"

She glanced at Whit. He started to say something and hesitated.

"I'll stay put this time," she said, guessing what was on his mind. "Promise."

By late afternoon the baby was growing more irritable.

"The fever's gone, but I think the rash is driving her crazy," Carly said. "We could use an oatmeal bath and lotion to calm that itch down or she's not going to sleep tonight."

Which meant none of them were sleeping, and Whit needed a few solid hours of rest to be sharp, to be able to protect Carly and Mia. He was already working at a disadvantage with the gunshot wound, and concussion, plus weakened muscles on his right arm from his previous injury. He didn't need to be cognitively impaired because of lack of sleep.

"We could ask Trish if she has lotion," Carly said.

"I'd rather keep the baby's condition to ourselves. That way if the innkeepers are asked, they can answer truthfully. I'll take you to the store."

"Are you sure?"

"I'll check with Deputy Logan to see if anyone reported the suspect's vehicle in town. He's probably long gone." At least Whit hoped he was.

Whit called the deputy, who said someone reported seeing the vehicle ten miles out of town. Deputy Logan also offered to escort Whit and Carly to the store.

"That was nice of him," Carly said.

"Yes, it was. Things are pretty quiet in a small town like Cold Creek Springs, so he's able to offer support to a fellow cop. Anyway, we could pick you up some clothes while we're out."

"Uh, like where? Shopping malls are hours away."

"Logan said there's a general store not far from here. They should have everything we need. I might even suggest you color your hair, if you're not opposed to the idea."

"The last time I tried that it turned out lime green."

"That wouldn't be good."

Carly almost smiled at the recollection. Good, at least he'd started to bridge the gap between them.

She picked up the baby and Mia whimpered as she stuck her thumb in her mouth. "We'll fix it, sweetie. Don't worry."

Whit had no doubt that Carly knew how to fix whatever ailed the child. Carly knew how to take care of Mia, something Whit would obviously fail at. Wasn't that one of the reasons his relationship with Pamela fell apart? Because he'd not so subtly let her know that he wasn't a kid kind of guy?

"I need to put my sweatshirt on." Carly handed Whit the baby.

He froze, his arms locked by his sides.

"Oh, I'm sorry. Your arm's bothering you?"

"No, it's okay." He took the baby, expecting her to fuss because of the awkward way he held her.

Mia blinked her bright blue eyes at him, and then pressed her cheek against his shoulder. He started to sway—he wasn't sure why—and a kind of warmth filled his chest that he'd never felt before. Mia made a humming sound. The vibration triggered a whole new set of emotions and feelings he couldn't find words to describe.

Carly put on her sweatshirt and shot him a curious look. He didn't want to let the baby go.

"I'll put together the diaper bag," she said.

"Take your time."

As they drove to the general store, Whit caught Carly watching him from the back seat.

"Yes?" he said in a light tone.

"Are you firing me?"

He sighed. "No, Carly. Mia needs you."

I need you. Whoa, back up.

Whit *did* need her, only not like *that*. He needed Carly to care for his niece and help him find Harry.

"Would you do me a favor?" Whit said.

"If I can."

"I understand that you want to keep your past to yourself, but could you warn me about stuff before it randomly pops up, like the restraining order business?"

"Okay."

He waited, hoping she'd share something else with him.

"Can I ask you a question?" she said.

"Yes."

"Why did you think it was your fault that Mia wasn't eating this morning?"

"In case you hadn't noticed I'm not good with kids."

"You seem like a natural to me."

He didn't know how to respond to that one.

"Did something happen?" she said.

"What do you mean?"

"Something with kids that would make you think you're not good with them?"

"You could say that."

He kept his eyes trained on the road. As a few minutes passed, he wondered if confessing his mistake might help her understand the dynamics of their family, and perhaps inspire her to share more of her own troubled past.

"I messed up when I was a teenager and Harry was seriously hurt," Whit said.

He glanced in the rearview mirror and saw her curious expression.

"He's okay now, as an adult." She paused. "So did he blame you for—"

"He didn't have to. It was my fault. I excel at taking care of myself, no one else." He regretted speaking the words the moment they left his mouth.

"I'd have to disagree," Carly said. "You've taken care of me and Mia for the past thirty-six hours, and you're suffering from a gunshot wound and concussion."

"It's my—"

"Don't say it's your job. That's a cop-out and you know it."

He shot her a quick glance, and then redirected his attention to the road.

"You've created this 'my job' wall to protect yourself," she said. "Being a good uncle isn't your job, Whit. You do it because you love your niece."

"I hadn't even met her until yesterday."

"That's a shame, truly. I hope you and your brother mend your relationship when this is all over."

"Me, too."

Her assessing stare made him uncomfortable, so Whit decided to turn the conversation around. "You're pretty good at building your own walls."

"Am I?"

"People are shooting at you, and police suspect you of being an accomplice to a kidnapping gone wrong, yet you won't share details of your criminal charges to ease everyone's suspicions."

"I don't need to explain myself. God knows my sins and He's forgiven me."

"Yeah, okay," he said, a little more clipped than he'd intended. He doubted his sins could be forgiven.

"I'm ashamed," she said suddenly.

"Because of your crime?"

"No, because I failed to protect my sister."

He couldn't bring himself to look at her.

"Ironically, it sounds like you and I have that in common," she said.

"Is she okay?" he asked.

"I don't know."

This time he glanced at her through the rearview. She was gazing out the back window with the saddest expression he'd ever seen.

"I'm sorry," he said.

"Yeah, me, too."

The rest of the trip was a silent one. He wanted Carly to explain her comment about not knowing how her sister was doing. At least Whit had been able to work his way back into Harry's life last year. It had been a slow reconciliation, one that taught Whit to be patient.

Patience was what he needed with Carly. He wanted her to consider him a friend, not an enemy. After the way he'd acted earlier, he knew it would be an uphill trek to gain her trust.

He pulled into the parking lot of Stratmore's General Store and spotted a patrol car. Deputy Logan got out and joined them.

"Thanks again for offering to keep an eye out," he greeted the deputy.

"No problem. It's a slow night. Ma'am," he greeted Carly.

"Officer."

Carly felt uncomfortable with a uniformed policeman escorting them into the general store. Walking beside him brought back too many memories, like the time she'd been caught stealing and the cop made her return the items and apologize to the clerk. She'd been confused and ashamed, and now realized that was probably the first time she experienced conflicted feelings about stealing, which was the family business. Her parents said it was okay to take things from people who didn't need them as much as Carly and her family.

A gentle hand snapped her out of the memory. "You okay?" Whit asked.

She nodded that she was but couldn't find the words to explain the knot in her gut.

As they entered the store, a bell jingled above the door announcing their presence.

"I'll stay here and keep watch," Deputy Logan said.

"Thanks," Whit said.

The store was larger than she expected and had a variety of goods, including women's clothes and even shoes.

She grabbed items and placed them in the cart

Whit pushed behind her. "This is quite a place, isn't it?" she said.

"Yep," Whit said, scanning their surroundings. "What else do we need?"

Carly listed off a few things and they made their way up and down the aisles. "More acetaminophen, oatmeal bath and anti-itch lotion."

They paused in front of a display of lotions. Whit's phone vibrated.

"Whittaker," he answered. "Okay, sounds good. I appreciate it."

A slight smile touched the corner of his lips and Carly wished she could have put that smile on his face.

"Thanks again. Bye."

"Everything okay?" Carly asked.

He looked straight at her. "Yep, it's all good."

Deputy Logan poked his head down their aisle. "Whittaker?" He motioned to Whit.

Whit glanced at Carly. "I'm fine," she said. "There's no one else here."

"I'll be right back." He disappeared around the corner and she heard low rumblings of male voices, then the jingle of the bell above the door. Deputy Logan had taken Whit outside to have a discussion? About Carly?

Stop being paranoid. This may not even involve you.

She couldn't stop herself from worrying, from

racking her brain for other things from her past that could rise up and rattle her relationship with Whit.

Relationship. Yes, they had one. They bonded over the love of a younger sibling.

She added anti-itch lotion, pain reliever—for both Mia and Whit—and oatmeal bath into the cart. A display of bandages caught her eye and she grabbed a few gauze bandages for Whit's injury. It hadn't bled through his shirt. However, that didn't mean it wasn't festering.

Mia suddenly spit up her dinner all over herself and Carly's jacket. Mia didn't like messes and started whimpering her displeasure.

"It's okay, sweetie." Carly went around the corner and spotted Whit talking with Deputy Logan through the front window. She got his attention, motioned to the mess on her shoulder and pointed to the bathroom sign. Whit nodded that he understood, his expression serious. Oh, man, she hoped it wasn't bad news about Mr. and Mrs. B.

"We'll get you cleaned up, little girl." They entered the ladies' washroom and went to the sink. Carly moistened a burp rag and wiped food off Mia's chin and cheeks.

"See, all better?"

Carly glanced into the mirror.

A woman stood there, gripping a weapon in her hand.

EIGHT

"Please don't hurt the baby," Carly said, keeping her back to the stranger.

The young woman cocked her head slightly as if puzzling over Carly's reaction. Then her gaze drifted down to her own hand.

"Oh, sorry. It's just a Taser."

Just?

"What do you want?" Carly blurted out.

"You're so good with her," the woman said softly. "I... I'm no good with kids."

Carly didn't know what to say. The woman's demeanor had suddenly shifted from aggressive to remorseful.

"Who are you?" Carly said.

"I'm her mom, her biological mom."

Carly's jaw must have dropped because the young woman continued, "You didn't know they adopted her?"

Carly shook her head.

"The Bremertons seemed like good people."

"They are good people," Carly said.

"Good people aren't kidnapped at gunpoint, unless they're into something criminal."

"You know about the kidnapping?"

The woman nodded.

"How did you find us?"

"I've been monitoring the police scanners. I heard the call go out about the doctor's office and have been following you ever since. I wanted to get you alone, to talk."

"I'm Carly," she introduced. "The nanny."

"Sam," the woman offered. "You guys should come with me."

It was a suggestion, not a threat.

"Why?" Carly said.

"Because you're obviously not safe."

"We're pretty safe. Mia and I are travelling with a police officer."

"That might not stop them."

"Who?"

"I'm not totally sure."

"Well, at least talk to my cop friend."

"No, thanks. Me and the cops…" Sam shook her head.

"I used to be the same way until recently. You can trust Whit."

"I'll pass." Concern creased her forehead. "I don't want you to think I'm a criminal or anything. I'm a coder and got caught up in something. The feds want to talk to me."

"So, you're like a black hat?"

Sam frowned. "No, nothing like that. I have scruples. My former employer did not."

"A bad guy, huh?"

"The worst."

"Do you think he has something to do with the kidnapping?"

"I hope not, or we're all toast."

We? Which meant Sam feared for herself, as well?

Someone tapped on the bathroom door. "Carly?" Whit's muted voice called. "Everything okay?"

The young woman straightened at first, and then leaned against the wall, resigned.

In that split second, Carly had to make a decision. There was something about Sam's expression as she studied Mia...

"Be right out!" Carly called to Whit.

Carly and Sam eyed each other and an odd sort of understanding grew between them.

"You're confident your cop friend can protect Mia?" Sam said.

"Yes. He's not just a cop. He's her uncle. I wish you'd talk to him."

Sam ignored the request and pulled out her phone. "Can we exchange numbers, so I can check on Mia once in a while?"

"Sure." Carly gave Sam her number.

"I'll text you mine."

"Sounds good."

Sam reached out and almost touched Mia's shoulder but didn't. "Take good care of her."

"I will."

"Thanks for not telling your friend about me. Here." Sam placed the Taser on the washbasin. "Never hurts to have one of these."

Sam went to the window and tossed her backpack outside.

"May the grace of the Lord be with you," Carly offered.

Sam cast a quick glance over her shoulder and disappeared into the night.

Carly was acting…strange. No matter how many times Whit asked if she was okay and how many times she answered that she was, he still felt like she was keeping something from him.

Yet he'd received the call from Megan back at the store that Carly's record was clean, even though her parents were serving time for fraud and embezzlement. That news supported Carly's story and eased Whit's worry over his new friend.

Friend? Was that what Carly was?

It didn't help that she was sitting in the back seat where he couldn't see her eyes. She'd chosen to ride in the back to comfort Mia, who was a little cranky.

They were halfway back to the inn when Carly suddenly said, "Whit, I need to tell you something and I'm pretty sure it will upset you."

"Okay."

"Something happened back at the store."

"Something as in…?"

"A woman approached me."

"Where?"

"In the bathroom. She said she was Mia's biological mother."

Whit snapped his attention to the rearview. "Did she threaten you?"

"No."

"Did she have a weapon?"

"She was carrying a Taser to defend herself."

"From what, you and a baby?" Whit's mind raced with worry. "Wait, she said she was Mia's mother?"

"Yes."

"So, she was a nutjob or something."

"Actually, I believed her."

"Carly—"

"I'm telling you what happened."

"Now, now that we're fifteen minutes away and she's long gone."

"I encouraged her to talk to you, but she refused."

"How did she even find us? Hang on. Was she in the bathroom when I knocked on the door?"

Carly hesitated. "Yes."

"And you didn't say anything?" He must have spoken a little too loudly because Mia squeaked. "Sorry." He lowered his voice. "Carly, what were you thinking?"

"I knew she wasn't going to hurt me, especially because I was holding her daughter in my arms."

"Do you know how crazy that sounds? Mia is Harry and Susan's child, not some random woman's kid."

"Sam knew the Bremertons and she knew about the break-in. She wanted to protect Mia and me from whoever is responsible for all this."

"And who's that?"

"She wasn't positive. It sounded like she had her suspicions."

"If she was telling the truth and she suspects who is after Mia, any rational person would have gone to the authorities for help."

"She doesn't have the best relationship with cops."

"Which should have been a clue she's not to be believed or trusted."

"I don't have the best relationship with cops and you trust me, at least with Mia, don't you?"

He ignored the question. Carly's role was... complicated.

"What were you trying to prove?" Whit said.

"I didn't feel threatened, and I know what that feels like. Besides, I figured it couldn't hurt to get more information about what's going on."

"And now she's gone."

"She has my number. She'll call to check on Mia."

Whit couldn't believe what he was hearing.

How could a woman with Carly's life experience be so naive?

"You know I'd never let anything happen to Mia," Carly said. "I was putting her needs first."

He squeezed the steering wheel tighter. "Wanna explain that?"

"If you and Deputy Logan had rushed in there, Sam might have panicked and tased someone and one of you would have shot her and all of that would have been dangerous for Mia. At least now we have a little more information about the situation."

"From an unstable stranger. Give me her description when we get back to the inn and I'll call it in."

Right after he called his tech to have her find hospital records of Susan giving birth to Mia.

"You're doing it again," Carly said.

"Doing what?"

"Acting like a cop, not an uncle."

"I *am* a cop."

"Well, maybe you'd be better off thinking like an uncle."

"I said I was sorry for raising my voice. It makes me crazy to think that you and Mia were in trouble and I couldn't help because you lied to me."

"I didn't lie. I said I'd be right out."

"Splitting hairs."

Silence filled the car. He wasn't sure how to

get through to Carly and explain that it damaged their relationship when she kept things from him.

"I want to trust you, Carly," he finally said.

"And I, you. Can't you accept that I have good instincts and in that moment I trusted them, much like you would have trusted yours?"

He wanted to understand where she was coming from, why she chose to keep the stranger's presence a secret. Instead he was struggling with the thought of what could have happened. He wasn't able to see past his frustration and he'd keep his mouth shut until he could find the right words to make her hear him.

"Did you see Susan when she was pregnant?" Carly asked.

"No."

"Did you ever wonder why she and Harry never invited the family to the christening?"

"They…christened her?" That was news to Whit.

"Yes, shortly after they hired me. I came to the christening and cared for Mia during the party."

"There was a party," he said, his tone flat.

"A lovely party. At the house."

He thought about that for a few minutes, puzzling over why his brother wouldn't have at least invited their mom and stepdad to the christening. Sure, Harry had distanced himself from the family, yet he still spoke to Mom every few weeks.

"We aren't a religious family," Whit started. "Maybe Harry thought that wasn't our thing."

"I'm not totally surprised by the possibility of Mia being adopted."

"Why would you say that?"

"A few things. Mrs. B. didn't nurse the baby, even a little, and studies show that nursing helps build an infant's immunity. Plus, she didn't seem to be recovering from childbirth."

"Why would they keep the adoption a secret from the family?"

"Maybe it just never came up. You said you weren't close."

True. They weren't close because they couldn't talk about their personal truths, couldn't share their emotional pain and ask for forgiveness.

Well, that wasn't totally true. Years ago Whit had tried apologizing to his brother for not taking better care of him. Harry blew him off, acted like he didn't remember the incident. Although Whit wasn't a share-your-feelings type of guy, he understood the importance of being honest and open with people you cared about, people who were important in your life.

In this case, Carly Winslow.

"I can't fail my brother again," Whit admitted.

"I understand."

"That's why it upsets me that you didn't let me know you were in trouble."

"I wasn't, Whit, honest. I—" she hesitated "—I felt sorry for Sam."

"Why?"

"You didn't see the look in her eyes. She was so broken and sad."

He suspected the woman reminded Carly of herself on some level except that as Carly made a credible argument for her actions, she didn't seem broken and sad. She sounded strong and determined.

You know I'd never let anything happen to Mia.

He couldn't argue with that. He might be frustrated beyond words, but he knew in his heart she was devoted to his niece.

So why was he still upset about her choice not to call out for his help?

He wanted to be the one to save her and Mia, to protect them. By doing so, he could potentially find some semblance of redemption for failing his brother.

He could be the honorable protector, not a self-centered jerk.

"You trust my love for your niece, right?" she asked.

"Yes."

"Good." She sighed. "That's what counts."

Whit wanted more. He wanted to trust Carly implicitly, especially if they were going to act as a team in order to protect Mia.

This tension between them was due to Whit not

fully trusting her and wanting to play hero, wanting to protect Carly and Mia on his own. Wasn't that in itself a selfish, ego-driven motivation?

He started questioning everything from his own motivations to Carly's actions. It was times like these he wished he had access to God so he could pray for guidance and listen for the answers. He admired that about Carly, and wondered if her faith had anything to do with her calm nature when confronted by the stranger.

"You're awfully quiet," she said.

"My head hurts." The concussion had triggered a dull headache he'd been unable to shake for hours.

"I bought extra pain reliever for you."

He heard her rustling in a bag.

"Let's wait until we get back to the inn," he said.

"Okay. I'll redress your wound, as well."

Even after he'd berated her for tonight's actions, she still offered to tend to his injury. He wasn't sure he would be so compassionate if their roles were reversed. And why had he berated her? For protecting his niece from a stranger and hoping to get information that could help authorities find his missing brother and sister-in-law?

Whit needed to stop trying to be the hero and accept the possibility that Carly was a solid ally, that she could be trusted.

"Weren't you scared?" he said.

"Of Sam?"

"Yeah."

"No, we made a connection. I could see the love in her eyes for Mia."

Love. That was Carly's barometer. That's how she found her truth, and ability to trust.

Whit's cell phone rang and he hit the answer button on the radio.

"Whittaker."

"It's Harper. You alone?"

"No, I've got Carly and the baby with me."

Harper hesitated.

"What is it?" Whit said.

"Your sister-in-law was involved in raising millions of dollars for Serenity Resort, filed as a nonprofit corporation. Something doesn't add up and she's under investigation by the feds."

"What are we looking at here?"

"Suspected fraud. According to the feds, money was transferred out of the official bank account into a Cayman Island bank a week ago."

"Did Susan transfer the money?"

"Can't confirm that," Harper said. "Also, the female kidnapper's minivan was stolen, so that's a dead end. How are things with you?"

"A woman claiming to be Mia's biological mother found us…well, found Carly."

"The baby's adopted?"

"Not sure. Thought you should look into that angle," Whit said.

"We also found the SUV Miss Winslow described as the one parked in front of the house the day of the break-in. It was abandoned in a random subdivision."

"And?" Whit felt he was holding back.

"There was blood in the back seat, torn clothing. Forensics is on it."

"Anything else?"

"Not at present. You feel safe where you're at?"

"Relatively."

"Keep in touch."

"Thanks." Whit ended the call. He'd feel safe when the case was solved and they found his brother. Alive.

There was blood in the back seat, torn clothing.

Reality hit him like a sucker punch to the gut: his brother might be dead or, at the very least, critically injured.

No, he couldn't go there.

Carly's gentle hand pressed against his shoulder, sending a wave of calm through his chest.

"Let's pray."

Back at the inn, Carly gave Mia an oatmeal bath, which seemed to ease the itch, and dabbed the child's skin with lotion. Singing softly, she rocked Mia and placed her in the crib.

She quietly went into the second bedroom, where Whit sat at the desk next to the window. He seemed deep in thought as he studied his tablet.

"She's asleep," Carly said.

He glanced up, tension creasing his forehead.

"Do you want me to redress your wound?" she said.

"I did already."

"Oh, okay. Did you take a pain reliever for—"

"Yes, when we got home."

Home. She didn't correct him. She'd often dreamed of living in a home with a principled man who loved her, despite her background, and cared for her and their children. Aunt Vicky had reminded Carly, *Our traumatic life experiences shape who we are. You've learned from yours and have become a wonderful woman.*

Since Whit was focused on whatever he was reading, Carly grabbed the shopping bag and started for the bathroom. He hadn't spoken much since she'd offered to pray in the SUV, and she hoped he wasn't upset that she'd suggested it. Sometimes people were uncomfortable praying, and even thought you were being condescending when you said you'd pray for them. Carly had wanted to offer Whit comfort because she sensed his desperation about his brother.

"Are you going to sleep?" he said.

She turned to him. "Not yet."

"Would you mind…talking for a while?" He shook his head slightly. "Never thought I'd hear those words come out of my mouth."

She went to the window seat next to the desk. "I'm sorry about before."

"Not telling me about the woman in the bathroom?"

"Well, yes, but also about praying in the car. I got the impression it made you uncomfortable."

"It didn't. It just felt—" he hesitated "—different."

"I sensed your pain and wanted to help. When I'm freaked out and don't know what to do, prayer helps."

"I envy that about you," he said softly.

"You shouldn't feel envious. You can do it, too. All by yourself. Well, not completely by yourself because God's there."

"Can I ask you a question?"

She nodded.

"Did this Sam woman give you any clue as to who she might be protecting you and Mia from?"

Carly sighed, thinking he was going to ask about God, not the case. "No, and I pressed her on it."

"She must have been keeping tabs on Mia if she knew about the break-in."

"I'd never seen her before, like when I was at the park with the baby."

"Tell me everything she said."

"She referred to herself as a coder. When I asked if she was a black hat, she seemed offended and said she had scruples, although her former employer didn't, and he was a brutal guy."

"You didn't get Sam's last name?"

"No."

"If she knew about the break-in, I'm thinking she tapped into the home video system." Whit glanced at her. "I'm assuming my brother had one."

"He did."

He redirected his attention to his tablet.

"Do you believe that Sam is Mia's biological mother?" Carly asked.

"I don't know what to think. I've done a cursory search and can't find evidence of Mia's birth to Susan and Harry."

It had been a long day and he looked completely drained.

"Why don't you get some sleep and I'll take care of Mia," Carly offered.

"I've got too many questions buzzing around in my brain, like who's got my brother and sister-in-law, and why they're after Mia."

"I know." Carly sighed. "I mean Mia is an innocent child."

"I'd like to think my brother is innocent, as well."

"I'm sure he is."

Whit glanced at her with bloodshot eyes. "What is he like as a dad?"

"He's amazing." She hugged her knees to her chest. "He always offers to hold Mia and lies on the floor to play with her. He makes these animal noises and she bursts into happy giggles. He's incredibly gentle and—"

A loud boom shook the windows and the lights went out.

NINE

Carly instinctively started for Mia's room and collided with Whit's hard chest. Apparently they had the same instinct. Get to the baby.

"Hang on a second." The soft blue glow of his cell phone lit his concerned face. He activated the flashlight app and pointed it toward the bathroom. "Stay close."

She not only stayed close, she gripped the belt loop of his jeans.

Mia, they had to get to Mia.

"Could be a random power outage," he said.

His suggestion didn't relieve her panic.

They made it through the bathroom and into the nursery, where he aimed the beam of light at the crib. Mia slept contently, a pacifier in her mouth.

"Thank the Lord," Carly whispered.

Another boom made Carly jerk. Whit put a firm arm around her shoulder.

"Whit—"

An alarm blared.

Carly grabbed the baby and wrapped her in a blanket. Whit led them to the door.

The hallway was filling with smoke.

A woman screamed as she ran past their door. It was Ingrid, Roger's wife. Roger was right behind her.

"Is the house on fire?" Roger said to Whit.

"Have no idea. Let's get downstairs."

Roger, Whit, Carly and the baby went quickly down the hallway, the smoke getting thicker, making Carly cough. She had to get the baby out of there. Fast.

They made it downstairs to the front door and out onto the porch.

Another scream echoed from the house. This time it wasn't Ingrid, who was trembling in her robe on the front lawn. Carly glanced at Whit. "The innkeepers?"

Whit handed her his truck keys. "You know what to do." He disappeared back into the house.

He wanted her to leave the premises.

To leave Whit behind.

Carly gripped the baby tighter and prayed for Whit's safety.

Talk about being pulled in opposite directions. Whit wanted to protect Mia and Carly, but he couldn't ignore the cries of a woman trapped by fire.

He raced into the kitchen, where a wall of

smoke blocked a closed door beside the refrigerator. That's where the woman's cries were coming from. He remembered the innkeepers saying
their room was off the kitchen. He pounded on
the door with a closed fist.

"Help!" Trish, the innkeeper, cried.

Whit carefully touched the doorknob. It wasn't
hot, so he turned it, but the door was locked.

"Unlock the door!"

No response. Had she succumbed to the smoke
and passed out?

Whit kicked the door open. "Trish!" He spotted her on the floor and helped her up. "Where's
your husband?"

"Not sure!"

"Who else is in the house?"

"Just your family, and Roger and his wife!"

"They're safe! Come on!"

He helped her up and out of the kitchen. As
they stumbled down the hall, she stopped short.
"What if Kurt's in the basement?"

"I'll check."

Covering his mouth with his shirtsleeve, Whit
led her down the hall and made sure she got outside.

He turned to go in search of Kurt. Halfway to
the basement door, someone tackled him, sending
him crashing into a table in the hallway. His attacker got Whit in a choke hold, probably hoping to
make Whit pass out and die from smoke inhalation.

No, Mia needed him.

Whit struggled to free himself, but his arms were weakened by his injuries. His strength was in his legs.

And his determination to protect his niece and Carly.

With a guttural groan, he pushed backward, banging his attacker into the wall and loosening the death grip on Whit's neck. Whit jammed his fist against the guy's nose and broke free.

Spun around to defend himself.

And was pistol-whipped.

Stars arced across his vision. The smoke was making it hard to breathe, to think.

Whit grabbed a lamp and swung it at the guy's head.

The gun went off.

Racing across the living room, Whit grabbed a wooden chair and broke a window.

Whit dived outside, landing on the side porch. Fighting to get air in his lungs, he scrambled away from the house.

Another shot rang out.

Whit didn't feel the burn of a bullet ripping through his flesh. It was just a matter of time, maybe seconds, before the shooter easily picked him off.

Leaving Carly and Mia vulnerable.

His head started to spin, and he collapsed on

the hard ground. No, he couldn't fail. Whit started to get up.

"Don't move!" a man shouted.

"What's the matter with you?" It was Carly's voice. Whit looked up. Carly stood protectively above Whit, clutching Mia in her arms.

She shouldn't be here. She should have left.

"Get away," he groaned.

"Roger, help me!" she called over her shoulder. The other inn guest helped Whit stand.

"Careful of the arm, he's injured," Carly said.

Injured? By now he should be dead. He'd counted two shots. It took only one to kill a man.

Roger helped Whit across the property to a nearby tree, where Whit collapsed, feeling weak and frustrated.

"The fire department is on the way!" Trish said, rushing over to them. "We have to contain this until they get here. Where's Kurt? Where's my husband?"

Carly's temper burned. "He was on the side porch threatening Whit with a gun."

"What?" Trish said, stupefied.

"There he is!" Roger pointed to the edge of the property where Kurt was doing something beside a large tank.

"He's trying to contain the fire," Trish said.

"I can't tell where it's coming from," Roger said.

"Come on!" Trish took off running, and Roger

followed. Ingrid stayed behind, blindly gazing at the house.

Carly swayed with Mia in her arms. The little girl was a trouper, able to sleep through anything.

Carly knelt beside Whit. "Where were you hurt?"

"Head."

"Were you shot?"

"Pistol-whipped. Did you say…it was Kurt? The owner of the inn?"

"That's who was standing over you with a gun, telling you not to move."

"We need to go."

"Relax. Let me take a look at your head." She eyed a bruise forming above his right eye.

"I'm confused," Whit said.

His weak voice worried her. She flashed two fingers. "How many fingers am I holding up?"

"Peace."

"You must be okay if you're joking around."

He squinted as if struggling to see her.

"You need a hospital."

"No hospital. We've gotta go." He started to get up and sat back down.

"Good choice."

In the distance, she watched Trish aim a hose at the kitchen area of the house, while Roger and Kurt took turns working some kind of pump. Carly didn't see a flame, just smoke.

"If the innkeeper is a part of this, we need to get out of here," Whit said.

Just then two police cars pulled up. One of the deputies joined the fire relief efforts, while the other approached Carly and Whit.

"You okay?" the deputy said.

"Yes, Officer," Carly offered.

Whit nodded.

"Are you Brody Whittaker?" the deputy asked.

Whit cocked his head. "Yeah."

"I'm Deputy Smith. Logan filled us in on your situation. You think this is related to the case in Miner?"

"Not sure. Looks like I was assaulted by the innkeeper, Kurt, which makes no sense."

"Once they contain the fire, we'll get everyone's statements and figure out what happened." With a nod, Deputy Smith went to help the others.

"What happened is we've been discovered and need to get out of here," Whit grumbled.

"Take it easy. No one's going to attack us with police here."

"I wouldn't be so sure," Whit said. "How's the baby?"

Carly glanced at Mia. "Perfect. I'm thankful she's oblivious to all this."

"Well, I'm thankful you're both okay." He eyed Mia with a strange expression. "I shouldn't have left you."

"You had to save Trish."

"Her husband was obviously inside."

"Well, he wasn't coming to her aid, so you did the honorable thing."

"Maybe."

"Maybe?" Carly questioned.

"Or I was trying to maintain my hero status."

"You aren't making sense."

"Harry once said it was more important for me to be a hero than to be a brother. Kind of like you saying it's more important for me to be a cop than an uncle."

"I never said you acted as if it were more important to be a cop. I said you get to choose, in any given situation, to put family first or your job first."

"Hopefully one day I'll make the right choice."

Carly didn't respond to that comment. She decided not to argue with a man suffering from a head injury. Whit's remark couldn't be further from the truth, at least from her perspective. He needed to save Trish, who could have died from smoke inhalation. Plus, he knew Mia was in good hands with Carly.

Whit wasn't the type of man who could walk away when someone needed him. At least that was Carly's take on Brody Whittaker.

She'd like to hold herself to that same high standard, which was one of the reasons she'd chosen to become a nurse. The fact that she hadn't been able to protect Greta when she needed Carly most still wore on her soul.

A few minutes later the fire trucks showed up. As the crew took over, Deputy Smith approached Carly and Whit, while the other deputy questioned the innkeepers and guests.

"The innkeeper found out you were using a false name," the deputy said. "He assumed it was because of criminal activity."

"How did he find out?"

"You used your credit card at the general store and he's friends with the clerk. Kurt was on the way back to confront you when he saw the smoke. By the way, there was no actual fire. Someone planted smoke devices in the HVAC system and set off an explosive device to cut the electricity."

"To get us outside," Whit said under his breath. "Then why did Kurt assault me inside the house?"

"He claims that wasn't him, that he only saw you when you jumped out the window onto the porch."

"Which means the perp could still be inside," Whit said.

"Unlikely. It's been cleared."

"He could still be around." Carly protectively held Mia and scanned the property.

Another car pulled up the driveway and Deputy Logan, in civilian clothes, joined them. "I heard the call go out."

"The assailant might still be on the premises," Smith said. "I'm calling the desk sergeant."

He stepped away and Deputy Logan stood protectively near Whit and Carly.

"How did they find us again?" Carly said.

"Phones?" Logan suggested.

"Location services are off," Whit said. "Maybe they figured out what I'm driving and are tracking my truck." He looked at Carly. "What I don't get is that you were out front with Mia, which was the perfect chance to take the baby. Why come inside after me?"

"Well, I wasn't alone. Roger, Ingrid and Trish were with me."

"Maybe they were trying to get you out of the picture for good," Logan suggested to Whit. "Without your protection, you two—" he nodded at Carly and Mia "—would be easy targets."

Whit nodded, and Carly wondered if puzzling through all this was irritating his concussion.

"You should have the paramedics look at you," she said.

"No time. We need to keep moving," Whit said.

"Where to?" Logan said.

"Anyplace we can't be found," Whit said. "We need to figure out how they tracked us here."

"I can check for tracking devices on your vehicle."

"That would be great. In the meantime, we have

to consider that the perp who assaulted me inside the house is watching us plan our next move."

The fire captain approached them. "No structural damage to the house. As we suspected, just smoke, no fire. Should be cleared in an hour."

"Thanks," Whit said, then looked at Deputy Logan. "Don't suppose you know where I can get cheap wheels for the next few days."

A few days? Carly appreciated his optimism about the amount of time it would take to resolve things, find the Bremertons and finally put an end to the violence.

"I do, actually," Deputy Logan said. "You thinking of abandoning your truck?"

"Temporarily."

Logan glanced across the property at Whit's vehicle. "I've always wanted to try one of those out."

"If they're tracking it that means they'll be following you," Whit warned.

"I'll park it at the station and drive my cruiser home. Neighbors like seeing the squad car out front anyway. You want to take my car for a few days?"

"It has to be a completely random car. No connection between me and the owner."

"I might have some ideas for you there. Can't do anything until morning, though. The three of you should spend the night at the station. You'll be safe there."

* * *

The door creaked open and two men in clown masks entered the small room. They stood over Harry and Susan, the silence deafening.

Was this it? The end? *Lord, I'm not finished.*

"I've changed my mind," the lead clown said. "I'll take your money."

"It's yours," Harry said. "As much as you want. All of it."

A few seconds passed.

"Take her."

The other guy grabbed Susan and pulled her up.

Harry reached out. "Wait, what are you doing?"

"Making sure you don't alert anyone to your whereabouts when you transfer the money."

"I wouldn't do that." Harry tried pushing past the thug.

The guy punched Harry in the gut. He doubled over, gasping for breath.

"I make the rules." The guy leaned close. "If you don't follow them, this is what happens."

He shoved a cell phone in Harry's face. A video image of smoke spewing out of a large house filled the screen. "Your daughter was in that house."

"Mia," he groaned.

"Bring the laptop," the kidnapper said to his associate.

A few minutes later Harry was transferring millions into a random offshore account. The lead clown closed the laptop and handed it to the other guy.

Harry leaned against the wall. "My daughter…?"

Someone tapped on the door and cracked it open. "Gus lost them," a man's voice said.

The lead clown slugged the guy. Harry heard him hit the ground, coughing.

"Idiot. I ordered him to wait," the lead clown said.

"I know," the man said in a raspy voice. "He was trying to make up for—"

"No excuses!"

From his stance, it looked like the lead clown was pointing his gun at the guy.

"Please, boss, we'll find them."

There was a hesitation, and then the leader lowered his weapon and shut the door. He turned back to Harry, who dreaded the physical abuse he was about to take from this maniac, but Harry's own discomfort was nothing compared with his worry about Susan and Mia.

The clown squatted next to him. This was it. Harry was about to get a bullet to the head. The kidnapper had gotten what he wanted—all of Harry's money, or at least everything that was liquid.

"About your wife," the kidnapper said.

Dread whipped through Harry's chest. Susan was dead.

"I've decided to release her."

Harry wanted to believe him but suspected this was another way to mess with Harry's head.

"Thank you." Harry played along.

The man burst out laughing and stood. "Oh, I'm not letting her go out of the goodness of my heart. We need to find the little girl. And where your wife goes, the daughter will follow."

"Mia was never in that burning house?"

"Oh, she was there." He stood and crossed the room. "But she's vanished, thanks to your cop brother. He's a real thorn in my side, but not for long."

The guy shut the door, leaving Harry alone.

"Way to go, Whit," he whispered.

They'd be safe? At a police station? Ironic, Carly thought as she sat on a cot next to Mia, giving her a morning bottle. Carly had kept a close watch of Mia all night for fear she might roll over and off the cot. Carly didn't sleep much, except when Whit demanded he take over so she could rest.

Carly couldn't sleep surrounded by bars. Last night at the inn she'd started to protest the suggestion they spend the night at the station, knowing that would mean sleeping in a cell. It turned out to be the best solution, even if that meant she'd have to relive her trauma in the worst possible way.

Somebody help me.

Why won't anyone help me?

They were the distant cries of a confused girl who'd been taken from her home for doing what she thought was right: protecting her baby sister, first from her mom, and then from police.

"Carly?"

She glanced across the cell at the open door. Whit stood there watching her. "You okay?"

Afraid she might snap his head off because of lack of sleep, she nodded and glanced at baby Mia. Placing an open hand on Mia's tummy, she thanked God that they'd been able to protect the child. It wasn't until this morning that Carly realized how exposed and vulnerable they'd been standing out in front of the inn. She'd been confident that nothing could have happened to them last night since they were surrounded by innocent bystanders, yet in the light of day she wouldn't put anything past the men who were after baby Mia.

Why? Why were they after this precious child?

Whit joined her on the cot and placed his hand over Carly's left hand, resting on her thigh. She didn't want his comfort. She wanted answers. She wanted this to be over.

She was done feeling vulnerable.

"Can you watch Mia? I need to stretch my legs." She stood and he held on to her hand.

"Where are you going?"

"To pace. I need to do something physical to shake all this gunk from my brain."

He released her hand. "Gunk?"

"Yes, gunk," she said, leaving the cell to pace in the hallway. She felt better already, just being out of the cage and moving around.

"You want to expand on that?"

"I like a calm environment. I also like to sing and read. I don't like fearing for my life, fearing for Mia's safety and being locked up in this place."

"We're not locked up. We can leave at any time."

"Only we can't because this is the safest place for us right now. I get it, I do, even if I don't like it."

"I guess I can see how being in here would make you feel bad if you'd done something wrong."

"I haven't done anything wrong, not now and not back then."

"I believe you."

She stopped short and narrowed her eyes. "Even though I was arrested?"

"Your record was expunged. That counts for a lot in my book. Besides, the way you've taken care of my niece these past few days, well—" he glanced at Mia "—it shows me what a good person you are."

That practically floored her. Carly wasn't used to a man being honest and kind...and complimentary. Her dating experience hadn't been all that successful, with her last boyfriend breaking up with her because he claimed she "mothered" him too much.

"You've only known me a couple of days," she said, sitting on the cot across the cell from him.

"I'm usually a pretty good judge of character." He smiled.

Her insides lit up like fireflies on a warm summer's night.

"Then again, I am suffering from head trauma," he teased.

"How can you still have a sense of humor when everything is such a mess?"

She wished she could be less serious and use humor to balance out her stress.

"Sorry, did my comment offend you?" he said.

"On the contrary, it made me smile and right now I didn't think anything could make me smile."

"I'm glad."

Tension eased from Carly's shoulders. Somehow she and Whit had developed a bond, maybe even a friendship, that brought her out of her spin zone.

The outer door opened and Deputy Logan joined them wearing a serious expression.

Whatever calm she'd felt from her and Whit's banter was immediately overshadowed by worry.

"What is it?" Whit said from the cell.

Logan glanced from Whit to Carly, back to Whit. "They found the child's mother, Susan Bremerton."

TEN

Silence filled the holding area. Whit couldn't bring himself to ask, fearing his brother was dead, even though the deputy hadn't mentioned him.

"Is she…?" Whit said, unable to complete his sentence.

"Alive."

Whit sighed with relief.

"Is she okay? Where did they find her? Does she know what it's all about?" Carly fired off. "Where is she now?"

"Back in Miner at Franciscan Health Center."

"What is she being treated for?" Carly asked.

"They can't share that information."

"But she's alive," Whit said, hoping that meant his brother was, as well.

"Yes, she's alive."

An hour later they were headed back to Miner to see Whit's sister-in-law. He was able to buy a used car from a friend of Deputy Logan's so they wouldn't be spotted when they got to Miner.

He reconsidered his decision to return to Miner, but Mia's mother had been found and he needed to reunite Susan with her child.

Her adopted child?

Another claim needing to be confirmed.

"I can't even imagine what she's been through," Carly said softly.

Which sparked his imagination about what they were doing to Harry. *Hang in there, little brother.*

Carly interlaced her hands, bowed her head and whispered something.

"Would you… Can I listen?" he said.

She looked sideways at him. "Of course." She closed her eyes and took a deep breath. "Lord, we pray for Mrs. Bremerton's recovery and for Mr. Bremerton's safe return. We pray for You to keep watch over him during this turbulent time. Amen."

"Amen," Whit whispered.

She was right. It did seem to ease the tightness in his chest.

"Thank you," he said.

"Of course. Do you think Detective Harper will be waiting for us at the hospital?"

"Yes. I hope he has more information about the kidnapping and leads on my brother's whereabouts." Whit gripped the steering. "Right now, the thought of losing my brother…" His voice trailed off.

"Don't go there."

"You said we have that in common, wanting to protect our siblings. When was the last time you saw your sister?"

"Fourteen years ago. The day my parents sent me to live with my aunt."

"They sent you away?"

"Yep."

"Why?"

"I was arrested, remember?"

He shot her a look.

"You really want to hear this?" she said.

"I really do."

She took a long, deep breath as if finding the courage to tell him her story. "I had finished Restorative Justice, written letters of apology, gone to group therapy sessions, etcetera. By doing these things my record would be expunged. My parents liked that, mostly because having a kid with a record would reflect poorly on them."

"If you did everything required of you, and your record was expunged, why did they send you to live with your aunt?"

"My parents said I needed to get out of town because I had a target on my back, that local police would be gunning for me."

"Uh…that's not how it works."

"My parents can be very—" she paused

"—convincing. Mom said she'd send for me in a few months. Never did. I hitchhiked back home. She was angry and took out a restraining order to keep me away from Greta."

"On what grounds?"

"She claimed she wanted to prevent my delinquent influence on my sister. It was another way to control me. She promised to withdraw the order if I went back to live with Aunt Vicky. I think Mom was afraid I'd eventually convince authorities of what my parents were into. She wanted me out of their lives."

The car went silent for a few minutes.

"That's awfully harsh," Whit said.

"I've accepted the fact that some people are, well, not good people. Like my parents. They threw me under the bus in order to protect their fraudulent business activities. No one listens to a juvenile delinquent."

"By the way, I found out your parents are currently serving time in Kansas."

"Doesn't surprise me. They swindled people out of thousands of dollars, all while maintaining their loving suburban couple image. Dad owned a marketing company and Mom was a housewife, although she barely took care of her house or her children."

"But there had to be a credible threat to get a restraining order."

"Well…" She hesitated. "I was arrested for felony menacing after threatening police officers with a knife."

It was Whit's turn to glance sideways at Carly.

"I would do anything to protect my baby sister." Her voice hitched. "First from my mom, who was teaching her how to steal, then from police, who were going to take Greta away from us."

"Police knew about your parents' illegal activities?"

"Nope."

"Then why would they take Greta away?"

"I'm not sure they would have. You've got to understand, Mom had been brainwashing me for years. 'Don't talk to police. Ever. About anything.' It didn't help that I'd been picked up a few times for shoplifting and brought home by local cops. Stealing was one talent I did not inherit from my parents, thank the Lord."

Whit felt terrible about this woman's history. What kind of parents would brainwash their kids into being afraid of cops?

"What compelled you to threaten cops with a knife? Can you…are you comfortable talking about it?"

She leaned back in the seat and crossed her arms over her chest. "I caught Mom working with Greta, teaching her how to snatch something out of a purse. She was only seven. I lost it and said Greta shouldn't be doing that. I locked myself and my sister in my bedroom. Mom shouted and pounded on the door. Greta was crying but wanted to stay with me. Then it got super quiet. A few minutes later Mom said through the door that neighbors had called police because they heard us yelling at each other, and heard Greta crying. 'Don't let them take Greta!' she pleaded with me, and apologized for our fight. Oh, man, she had laid it on thick and knew how to push my buttons. When the cops broke down the door, I held on to Greta with one hand and waved a kitchen knife with the other."

"You kept a knife in your room?"

"Mom conveniently slid it under the door after telling me the police were coming to take Greta away."

The car grew oddly quiet.

"Now that I'm retelling the story I can hardly believe it myself. That's how it happened, or at least how my thirteen-year-old mind remembers it."

"Did you explain this to police?"

"I was brainwashed, remember? Besides, they did in fact take Greta away from me. I was so scared, convinced they would destroy our family." She sighed. "A nice social worker persuaded me to tell her the truth. It still didn't convince police. After all, I had a record of petty theft and truancies, and I was telling stories about my successful father and supposedly loving mother."

"If your dad had a successful business, why commit fraud?"

"The adrenaline rush? I don't know. He was gone a lot so I didn't have much of a relationship with him."

"So you went back to live with your aunt."

"I did. She taught me how to believe in myself, to believe in God. She was so different from my mom. Aunt Vicky said Mom had been coerced by my father into criminal behavior. My aunt praised me for having such a strong character and fighting for Greta like that, for being my own person. That's the history of Carly Anna Winslow, formerly Garber."

"Thank you," Whit said.

"For what?"

"For trusting me with your story, even though I'm a cop."

"You're also Mia's uncle so you can't be all bad."

"Well, thanks."

She smiled. "You're welcome."

This easy conversation was new for Whit. It felt natural to communicate this way, which was saying a lot considering the topic of conversation: Carly's tumultuous past.

"Now I get why you're so protective of Mia," he said.

"Let's hope I don't mess it up this time."

"I don't think you messed anything up, Carly. You were a kid."

"I was a teenager who wasn't able to protect her little sister."

"How old would she be now?"

"Twenty-one. I went back to see her when I was eighteen and my family was gone. Not in the house, not even in the same city. It's like they never existed. I suspected they were close to being caught for something illegal and decided to start over in another town. I never saw my sister again."

"Did you consider hiring a private detective?"

"I did hire a PI. It's costly and neither my aunt nor I had unlimited funds to support that for very long. My parents excelled at disappearing. Then I wondered why Greta didn't try to find me. She knew I'd gone to live with Aunt Vicky, so she could have reached out. Perhaps she didn't want to reconnect because my parents had filled her mind with lies."

"You can't know that for sure."

"It's one possibility. The other is that she resented me for disappearing on her. Either way, I'm not sure the relationship is repairable."

Whit felt her pain. He'd be devastated if he'd never reconciled with Harry, which he was in the process of doing when all this happened.

Carly's story intensified his determination to find his brother. Whit needed to apologize and somehow resolve their differences, even if that meant taking whatever verbal lashing Harry felt he needed to get off his chest.

"You shouldn't give up," he said.

"I know. I guess that makes me a coward."

He snapped his attention to her. "You're not a coward, Carly. Look at everything you've done to protect Mia."

"It's my job." She gazed out the window with a wistful expression he wanted to wipe off her face.

"Hey, how can you say it and I can't?" he teased again.

She shot him a slight smile. "I'm just an employee, you're a family member."

"I doubt Mia sees it that way."

"I do love her like she's my own. How could you not?" She glanced over the front seat at the sleeping little girl.

"How was Susan with Mia?" he asked, wanting more information about his sister-in-law.

"She was—" Carly hesitated "—nervous, I guess? She loves Mia deeply, you can tell."

"Why nervous?"

"I don't know. It was almost as if she lacked confidence in her ability as a mother."

"Tell me more about her."

"Well, before she became a mom she was a brilliant businesswoman, so she took that experience and applied it to raising money for worthy causes. She doted on Mia when she was home, although she was gone quite a bit."

"She is no longer working?"

"No, Mr. B. said it would be too stressful."

Whit glanced at her in question.

"I hear things through the baby monitor," Carly said. "I try not to listen. Sometimes you can't help it."

"Actually, you overhearing their conversations might be the thing that helps us find my brother. Back to my sister-in-law…"

As Carly described Harry's wife, Whit considered why his brother had picked Susan to be his life partner. The thought of making a commitment like that made Whit uncomfortable, maybe because he'd seen how his mother's two marriages had failed. After she'd divorced Whit's dad, she'd married Harry's father, and they had Harry and Beth. That marriage fell apart when Harry was fourteen and Beth eleven, leaving both kids without a consistent father figure.

No wonder Harry had gotten into trouble as a teen. Yet as an adult it seemed like Harry had turned things around. He was a successful and wealthy businessman, a husband and a father.

Who, upon their first phone conversation in years, said he didn't need help from his older brother. Not anymore.

Now Harry *did* need his brother's help and Whit would be there for him. He'd protect Harry's child and rescue Harry from the kidnappers. They had to want something, right? After all, they'd released Susan. Whit hoped she wasn't critically injured and prayed she'd be able to shed light on what started everything in motion.

Prayed. Yes, that was the right word.

"Where are you?" Carly said, tucking a few blond strands of hair behind her ear.

"Excuse me?"

"You suddenly went far, far away."

"I was thinking about Susan, hoping she's okay. And, of course—" he hesitated "—thinking about my brother."

She touched his shoulder. "'Trust in the Lord with all your heart, and lean not on your own understanding.' That's from the Bible."

"Is my brother a religious man?"

"He is, yes."

"Then I guess it's worth a try."

Detective Harper was waiting for them at the hospital where Mrs. B. was being treated. As Whit, Carly and Mia approached a side entrance designed to keep their presence a secret, Carly noted that Harper's expression seemed softer.

"How are you guys holding up?" he asked, giving Carly a polite nod. He led them down the hallway toward an elevator.

"We're okay, but frustrated," Whit said. "Someone set off a smoke device at the inn, most likely to evacuate the house and kidnap the baby."

"But they didn't get her."

"No, they didn't."

"We uncovered evidence of the baby being adopted, so the woman you encountered might have been telling the truth about being the child's mother."

Whit shook his head.

"What?" Carly challenged.

"I just hope the adoption was legit."

Carly considered his words.

"Think you were followed back to Miner?" Harper asked.

"I made sure we weren't, although if they know Susan is here they'll assume we'll turn up eventually. How is my sister-in-law?"

"About that." Harper pressed the elevator button to the third floor. "She seems traumatized and isn't talking."

"At all?" Whit said.

"If you ask her where she is, she'll answer the hospital, or if you ask her age, she'll tell you," Harper said. "If you mention her husband and the kidnapping, she completely shuts down."

Carly read Whit's worried expression.

"Mia will get through to her, won't you, baby girl?" Carly said, shaking a small rattle. Mia's fingers sprung open and she grinned. Carly placed the rattle in her hand. "When Mama sees your smiling face everything will be A-OK."

"Where did you find her?" Whit asked.

"A truck stop ten miles north of town. She was

curled up in a blanket on the floor of the women's bathroom. Someone called the police and the deputy at the scene identified her from the BOLO."

The elevator door opened and anxiety whipped through Carly's chest. It had nothing to do with being around an injured person. After all, she was going to be a nurse, but Mrs. B. wasn't just any injured person. Would her broken appearance frighten Mia?

"Is she bruised or anything?" Carly asked.

"No physical injuries," Harper said. "Maybe you should go in one at a time."

Harper paused outside Mrs. B.'s room.

Whit motioned for Carly to go first. "She needs to see Mia. I'll be behind you but I'll stay out of sight."

Carly took a deep breath and headed into the room. The first bed was empty and the curtain was pulled closed for privacy.

"Mrs. Bremerton?" Carly stepped around the curtain.

Susan Bremerton stared straight ahead as if she didn't see or hear Carly.

Carly forced a smile and jiggled Mia's rattle. "Look who's here, Mrs. B. It's your baby girl." She approached the bed. Out of the corner of her eye, Carly saw Whit peer around the curtain.

Susan Bremerton's expression didn't change.

"We're so glad you're okay," Carly continued. "Mia's had quite the adventure. Here, would you like to hold her?" Carly offered Mia to her mom. When she didn't take her, Carly sat Mia on the bed beside her, supporting her from behind. Mia giggled and waved her rattle.

No response from her mother.

Then Mia decided to play the fall-down game. She squealed and fell forward. Mrs. B. instinctively reached out to catch her. She hesitated for a second, then pulled Mia into a hug.

"Big Mama hug," Carly said in a soft voice.

The baby squealed and kicked with delight. She loved hugs from her mama.

Mrs. B. closed her eyes and pressed her lips against Mia's head.

Carly's eyes misted with tears. No words could get through to Susan, but the love of her child pierced the fog.

A love Carly had never experienced with her own mother.

"Susan?" Whit said, slowly approaching.

"My baby, my baby girl," Susan whispered against Mia, ignoring Whit.

"You should be proud, Mrs. B.," Carly said. "Your little girl is so good, even at the doctor's office."

Mrs. B.'s eyes widened, and she finally focused on Carly. "Doctor?"

"Her cold turned into roseola and she developed a rash. I gave her an oatmeal bath and applied anti-itch lotion and she was a happy little princess." Carly smiled at Mia.

"You…you always know what to do," Susan said. "Thank you, thank you, Carly."

She was about to say it was her job to take care of Mia and caught herself. It was more than a job for Carly. She loved this little girl.

"Susan, I'm Harry's half brother, Whit. I'm glad you're okay," Whit said. "Can you tell us what happened?"

Mrs. B. acted as if she didn't hear his question and continued to love on her little girl. "My baby girl. Such a precious girl."

Carly and Whit shared a look. Either Mrs. B. was purposely ignoring his question because the answer was too devastating to recall, or she was mentally unstable.

Detective Harper approached the foot of her bed. "Mrs. Bremerton, where is your husband?"

Again, she didn't react to the question.

Carly figured she'd try, since Mrs. B. was responding to Carly's presence if not the two men standing there. "Mrs. B.?"

She looked over the top of Mia's head at Carly.

"Where is Mr. B.? Mia misses her papa."

"Isn't he here?" She glanced past Whit. "Harry? Harry, where are you?"

"No, ma'am, he's not here," Harper said. "Do you remember what happened? Someone broke into your house."

Mrs. B. looked at Carly for confirmation as if she'd heard Harper's words but they didn't register.

Carly nodded. "It's true. Someone broke in. I was upstairs with the baby and you were downstairs with—"

"Nooo! Harry!" she howled, startling Mia. The little girl's lips furled and she started crying. Mrs. B. motioned Carly closer, as if wanting to tell her a secret.

Carly leaned close.

"They want the baby," Mrs. B. said with a wild look in her eye. "Don't let them get my baby. Take her. Keep her safe." She handed Carly the baby, who continued to cry because of her mother's sudden outburst.

"Mrs. B.—"

"Go away!" she shouted. "All of you just go away. Harry," she moaned, turning her back to the men and sobbing. "What have I done?"

Whit came around to the other side of the bed and sat down. "Susan, please," he said softly. "I need to know… Is my brother alive?"

She nodded that he was.

"Is he—"

"Goooo!" She frantically punched the nurse call button. "I need the nurse, I need… I need Harry," she sobbed.

"I do, too." Whit placed his hand on her shoulder and she froze, looking at him with such devastation in her wide eyes.

"I need my brother." He offered a slight nod. "Help me find him?"

Silence filled the room. Carly soothed Mia by stroking her back, and Detective Harper stood by without saying a word. Carly sensed Mrs. B. was about to speak.

"What's going on in here?" a middle-aged nurse said, entering the room. "She's allowed one visitor at a time, and only if she's up to it. Susan, how are you feeling?"

Mrs. B. stared blindly across the room. It seemed like she had drifted into another world, and nothing was bringing her back.

"That's enough for today," the nurse said with a stern expression.

"I have to—"

"Sir," she interrupted Whit, "do I have to call security?"

He slowly stood, the color draining from his face. Carly had to look away from the sadness she read in his eyes.

Wanting to ease everyone's pain, Carly stepped into Mrs. B.'s line of vision. "Mia is so glad her mama's okay. We'll come back soon to visit, right, baby girl?"

On cue, Mia sighed.

"Such a good girl," Carly whispered and headed for the door.

There was nothing more they could do for Mrs. B. Not until the doctors were able to diagnose and treat her condition. Carly didn't doubt she'd been through a traumatic experience that caused her to shut down.

Don't let them get my baby! Take her. Keep her safe.

The memory of her plea intensified Carly's worry. How were she and Whit going to keep Mia safe when they still didn't know who was after them or why?

What have I done? Mrs. B. had said. Which meant she blamed herself for the kidnapping and threat to Mia.

"I don't get it," Whit said as Harper led them to a waiting area. "Why release Susan and not my brother?"

"Leverage?"

"For what?"

"Let's say she's involved in fraud or a Ponzi scheme and someone wants his money back. They failed to kidnap the baby, thanks to you and Carly, so what's the next best pressure point?"

Whit nodded. "My brother."

"Maybe they release Susan Bremerton and control her actions," Harper suggested.

"Right now it doesn't look like anyone is in control, not even Susan."

"At least we know your brother is alive," Harper said.

"According to a hysterical woman who floats in and out of lucidity."

"Positive thinking, Whit," Carly said. "If she said your brother is alive, I believe her. She's traumatized, not delusional."

"She's right," Harper agreed.

Whit glanced down the hall toward her room. "I want to talk to her again."

"I understand, but this is my job, okay?" Harper said. "I'll call if anything changes."

"How long will she be hospitalized?" Whit said.

"They won't release her until she's stable," Carly offered.

"I want to be close," Whit said.

Carly swayed with the baby in her arms. Mia had gotten a hold of her thumb and was sucking quietly.

"There are a few hotels nearby," Harper offered. "They'll probably look there first."

"What are our other options?"

"We're still processing the crime scene, so you can't stay at the house. Unfortunate because they'd never expect you to go back there, plus the police presence would give an added level of protection."

"What about the coach house over the garage?" Carly said.

They both looked at her.

"It's a two-bedroom suite with a kitchenette. Mr. B. built it for out-of-town guests."

"You mean like family?" Harper asked.

She hesitated, not wanting to hurt Whit's feelings. "Um, sure, and sometimes business associates stayed there."

"Not a bad option," Harper said. "I'll work on getting you police protection, although we have limited staff and I have assigned someone to Mrs. Bremerton 24/7."

"Like you said, they won't expect us to go back to the Bremerton estate," Whit said. "The entire property is gated and has a security system, right?" He looked at Carly.

"It does, although the kidnappers managed to get through."

"We think someone cloned Mr. Bremerton's phone and that's how they gained access," Harper said.

"We'll need to change the security pass codes," Whit said.

"I've got the contact information for the security company," Carly said. "It's 24/7 service."

"Good, let's give them a call."

An hour later they were settled in the coach house above the garage and across the driveway from the main house. Carly was relieved that the security company had been able to reprogram the access codes so no one could gain entry onto the property except the police, Whit and Carly.

Since Mia was making her hungry squeak, Carly sat her on her lap at the table and fed her a late-night snack of bananas and milk. The poor kid's schedule was all messed up.

"I'm sorry if this is hard for you," Whit said.

She glanced at him. "What do you mean?"

"Coming back to the house." He was standing guard by the window.

"I'm okay. What are you looking for?"

"Nothing."

"Are you worried we won't be safe?"

"No. The gates are locked and the security company will notify police if the system is breached. Plus, Harper was going to try to have a deputy cruise by periodically."

"Then why are you staring at the house?"

"I'm imagining my brother back in there with his wife and child, although Susan may not be coming home if she's committed a crime." He glanced at Carly and Mia. "Which means if Harry survives, he'll be raising his daughter alone, unless the biological mother appeals to get her back. After this mess she might have a case for Susan being an unfit mother."

"Whoa, slow down. You're getting way ahead of yourself. I know what you need."

"What's that?"

"Food." She got up and handed the baby to Whit. "And some baby love." He easily took Mia and held her close. Carly wanted to stand there for a minute to enjoy the sight of his large hands holding the seven-month-old so gently, but she didn't want him to grow self-conscious. She turned and went to the kitchenette. "They keep the kitchen stocked for guests."

"You actually have an appetite?" Whit said as Mia leaned against his shoulder.

"Yeah, sorry."

"Don't apologize. You're right. I should probably eat something." He swayed slightly from side to side.

"Bingo." She grabbed two cans of beef chili off a shelf and held them up. "You game?"

"Sure."

She opened the chili and dumped it into a pot. "I know once Mrs. B. gets better she'll be able to help police find your brother."

"How do you do that?" he said.

"Do what? Multitask?"

"Stay so positive all the time."

"What's the alternative?"

Mia fussed against Whit's shoulder.

"Here, I'll put her down," Carly offered.

"Okay, we'll swap and I'll warm up the chili."

She took Mia from his arms and carried her into the bedroom where they'd set up a portable crib they'd found in the closet.

Carly hummed and shifted from side to side, lulling the child to sleep. It usually took only a few minutes before Mia drifted off. Tonight was no different. Carly placed her on her back in the crib. Rubbing her tummy ever so slightly, Carly continued to hum.

How did she even know how to do this?

It's God's work.

It truly was, and she wondered if she would ever have the opportunity to comfort and love a child of her own like she loved Mia.

The lack of decent sleep these past few days must be catching up to her. Why else would she be thinking about the impossibility of being a mother, of sharing a life with…

A man like Brody Whittaker.

Yes, she was very tired.

As she watched Mia's chest rise and fall with each breath, Carly felt extremely present and at peace. If nothing else, she was able to give this child the love Carly had been storing up for years—for Greta.

"Sleep tight, little one. May the Lord bless you and keep you safe."

She tiptoed across the room, glanced at Mia one last time and carefully closed the door. "She's out."

Carly turned to an empty living area.

"Whit?"

Maybe he needed to get something from the car.

She went to the window where Whit had been standing and looked outside, unable to see much because of the inside lights.

She flipped off the lights, plunging herself into darkness.

Her heart rate sped up.

No, they were safe here. Even the police said they'd be safe.

Yeah, and since when did you believe the police?

Since she'd become friends with Whit.

A blinking light drew her attention to the downstairs office of the main house. Someone was inside.

Then she spotted the silhouette of a man walking toward the house.

Whit.

And he was heading straight into an ambush.

ELEVEN

Carly was in the next room with Mia when Whit saw it: the flicker of a flashlight coming from inside the house. He bolted outside and across the driveway. He should have let Carly know what was going on, but he didn't want to disturb the baby and couldn't wait for Carly to finish putting Mia to sleep.

Someone was in Harry's house.

How was that even possible? Whoever was inside might know Harry's whereabouts. Maybe Whit could use the intruder as leverage against his employer and threaten his life if they didn't release Harry.

Now who sounded like a criminal?

No, that wasn't Whit. It was anger and worry driving him to the house to nab the perp before he disappeared. The intruder had breached a crime scene. The guy had guts.

Or desperately needed something from inside. Whit flattened himself against the side of the house, edging his way toward the front door. They'd recoded that lock as well, so he'd be able to gain access. Police had supposedly set the alarm when they left tonight, so how did this guy gain access? And what was he after?

Whit let himself in and stepped into the large foyer. Listened.

Heard nothing.

He wouldn't accept the possibility that the perp, who could have answers about Harry, had fled the scene.

A noise echoed down the hall.

Whit approached the room slowly, silently.

He had no idea what he was walking into. A few more steps…

He popped into the doorway, aiming his firearm. "Freeze! Police!"

A silhouette of a figure dressed in all black darted outside through the French doors.

"Stop!" He chased after the intruder.

The perp sprinted across the property, disappearing behind a shed. Not good. Whit could be walking into an ambush, but he couldn't let the intruder get away.

Then again, if Whit was dealing with a violent criminal the guy would have just shot Whit on sight.

He reconsidered going after the perp without backup, but it was too late for second thoughts.

He had to continue his pursuit and find the guy who had answers about Harry.

"Come out of there!" he ordered.

Rustling echoed beyond the shed in the woods. Great, the perp was trying to flee the premises. With energy he didn't know he had, Whit pursued him deep into the forest. The full moon lit his way to a point, but once the glow was blocked by the mass of pine and cedar trees, Whit lost sight of the perp.

Using the trees as cover, he stopped and listened. More rustling echoed from the left about a hundred feet in the distance. Staying low, he headed toward the sound. He could barely hear his own thoughts through the pumping of his adrenaline.

He went deeper into the forest, ignoring the sting of various bushes and tree limbs as they slapped his face. Determination drove him into the darkness.

That rational voice in his head shouted that this was a bad move, that he was being lured into a trap, but emotion was driving him. The love he felt for his brother fueled Whit like high-octane gas in a race car.

A crunching sound suddenly drew his attention to the right. Was the guy lost, zigzagging through the woods because he didn't know where to go?

Or was he trying to lure Whit away from the house, away from…

"Mia," he whispered.

In that split second, he was shocked back to his senses. He was supposed to protect Mia and Carly, and instead chose to take off on a one-man mission to capture the intruder.

He'd left Carly and Mia alone and vulnerable.

Breathing heavily, he stopped short, spun around and took off toward the coach house. Was this the strategy all along? Distract him long enough to kidnap Carly and Mia? What a fool. He'd played right into his enemy's plan.

His only excuse was he was out of his mind, so worried about his brother that his common sense had shut down, and he'd lost his edge.

Sprinting across the property, he caught himself praying for Carly and the baby's safety. *Please, God, don't let my failure put them at risk.*

He turned a corner and saw the coach house in the distance. The lights were off.

"No," he ground out.

He couldn't run fast enough, afraid he was too late. They'd taken his niece. They'd taken Carly, a woman who fascinated him and warmed his heart with her faith and kindness. Her bright, light energy.

Extinguished. Because he'd abandoned her.

Blinded by panic, he scaled the coach house stairs two at a time. Unlocked the door.

Rushed through the living room to the bedroom. Turned on the lights.

The crib was empty.

Rage churned in his chest. "Carly!" The anguished cry burst from his chest.

"Whit?" a muffled voice said.

He straightened. Now he was hearing things?

The door to the closet cracked open. He opened it wider.

Carly was sitting on the closet floor with Mia stretched out beside her on a blanket. Carly was patting the child's tummy with one hand and gripping a Taser with the other.

"Where'd you get that?" he said.

"Sam gave it to me."

"Are you…okay?" he said.

She nodded that she was. He offered his hand and she took it. The warmth shot clear up his arm to his heart.

She was okay. Mia was okay.

He automatically pulled Carly into a hug. When he let go, she glanced questioningly into his eyes.

"We're really okay," she said. "Better now that you're back."

She tucked the Taser into her back pocket, kneeled and picked up Mia, who seemed to be sound asleep. Humming softly, Carly put the baby in the crib. She and Whit went to the living room.

"I shouldn't have left you," he said.

"I understand." Carly headed for the kitchenette. "You saw someone at the house, right?"

"That's not a good enough excuse to leave you two alone."

Pounding thundered up the stairs. Whit withdrew his gun and Carly aimed her Taser at the door.

Detective Harper froze in the doorway. "Uh… don't shoot?"

Whit and Carly lowered their weapons, Carly placing hers on the kitchen table.

"How did you—" Whit said.

"Carly called 9-1-1," Harper interrupted. "She reported someone broke into the house and you went to investigate."

"So much for changing the pass codes for security purposes," Carly said.

"They didn't come for the baby," Whit said. "This feels different. Why break into the house if what they wanted was Mia? They obviously knew she wouldn't be there."

"Did you get a good look at him?" Harper said.

"No, he took off before I could see his face although he was on the small side, maybe five-six or -seven?" Whit, still ashamed about his behavior, forced himself to look at Carly. "What room was the intruder searching?"

"Your brother's office."

"What were they looking for?" Harper said.

Whit shook his head. An acute headache was building behind his eyes and not because he'd chased a perp across the backyard. His head ached from all the questions plaguing him, questions like how they accessed the code so quickly, why they risked breaking into the house and the most important question: Was Whit the right man to be protecting Carly and Mia?

The answer to that last question was obvious.

He looked at Detective Harper. "Carly and Mia should go into protective custody. Immediately."

"What? No," Carly said.

Whit acted like he didn't hear her and continued to address the detective. "They'll be safe in the custody of people whose sole job it is to protect them."

"I thought that was your job," Harper countered.

"It *is* his job," Carly snapped.

"Harper, can you give us a minute?" Whit asked.

"Sure." He left the coach house and Whit closed the door.

With his back to her, Whit said, "You were right, Carly. I'm about the job first and everything else second. I left you two alone. I never should have done that."

"Whit, we're fine."

He turned to her. "You didn't look fine when I opened the closet door. You looked…"

"What?"

"I don't know, you looked scared and fragile and the baby—"

"Mia is fine."

"I'm responsible for that. I'm the reason you had to hide in a closet with only a Taser to defend you and the baby. I'm the absolute wrong person to be protecting you." He paced toward the refrigerator and pulled out a can of soda. "Let the professionals take it from here."

"You are a professional."

"I can't be objective."

"You don't need to be objective. You need to be an uncle. And you've done a fine job of that so far."

"I disagree. I abandoned you and the baby to go chasing after some guy. There could have been two or three of them and they could have overpowered me and found you and..." His voice trailed off.

She could tell he was slipping into that dark place and she had to stop it. She'd gone there plenty of times herself and it served no good purpose.

"They didn't find us," Carly said. "I'll say it again. We're fine. You're fine."

He shook his head. "You called it from the beginning. I'm incapable of being an uncle first and cop second. I'm all about myself, my ego. I'll accept that."

"Well, I'm not accepting it because it's not true."

"Carly—"

"Why did you go after the burglar?"

"Because he was breaking into the house and my cop instincts kicked in."

"That wouldn't be enough to tear you away from your niece. What were you thinking about when you went down there?"

"I wasn't thinking. That's the point."

"Let me try another way. What were you feeling?"

"That someone was breaking into my brother's house and I had to detain him."

"Why?"

"Because…because he might know where they're holding Harry."

"Okay, so maybe you were acting like a cop, but primarily you were thinking and feeling like a brother. Am I right?"

"What difference does it make? I left you alone."

"Snap out of it. You're her uncle and right now her mom and dad aren't able to protect her so you're the best thing she's got. You'd protect her with your own life if need be. So yes, in this case, right now, you are being selfish. You're wallowing in self-pity and you need to knock it off."

Whoa. Carly wasn't sure where she'd found the courage to speak her truth like that, but it felt good. Not good, amazing, like a weight had been lifted off her shoulders. It was draining to always say the right things, things people wanted to hear, as opposed to the direct truth.

From the expression on Whit's face, she'd definitely hit a nerve. He studied the soda clenched in his hand as if trying to come up with an appropriate response to defend himself.

Deep down, he knew she was right.

Carly shifted onto a kitchen chair. "I'm sorry if that was harsh, but your niece needs you. Don't pass her off to strangers."

"She'll be with you."

"Please don't pass me off to strangers."

He joined her at the table. "I was a stranger until two days ago."

"Well, considering our current situation, I'd say we're on the fast track to being good friends, wouldn't you?"

"Friends." He hesitated. "Yeah, it feels that way."

It felt like much more than a budding friendship to Carly. She reminded herself that the intense crisis they were embroiled in, plus the shared love of the little girl in the next room, was what created the strong bond between them. If Carly and Whit met on a blind date or even at church, they probably wouldn't give each other a second thought.

That wasn't completely true, Carly admitted. Something drew her to Whit beyond his good looks. There was an air of integrity about him that made her feel safe.

Another reason she wanted Whit to remain as her and Mia's protector.

"I trust you," she said. "That's unexpected considering my history with cops."

"Carly—"

"No."

"You don't know what I was going to say," Whit protested.

"I have a pretty good idea."

"You think you know me that well, huh?"

"I know you carry around a lot of guilt about your relationship with your brother. Is that why you want to dump us? Because Mia reminds you of that perceived failure?"

"No, and don't say that. I'm not dumping anybody."

"What would you call it? You'd be essentially handing us over to people who don't care about us—I mean Mia—the way you do. They're not as invested in our comfort or our safety as you are."

"Carly—"

"Just stop. I'm tired of arguing. I'm tired of this whole mess. I'm going to sleep." Not that she'd sleep much tonight. "Good night."

"I thought you were hungry."

"I'll eat tomorrow." She headed toward Mia's room. She didn't know what else to do and had to get away from Whit, both because she was frustrated and wasn't getting through his thick skull, and also because the thought of not seeing him again tore her apart.

She hesitated before opening the bedroom door, not looking at him. "I feel safe with you, Whit. I don't think…" She paused, reconsidering her confession. "I can't remember ever saying that to anyone."

She went into the bedroom, shut the door and began to pray.

Carly fully expected a sheriff's deputy to be in the coach house living room the next morning. After changing Mia's diapers and clothes, she opened the door and found Whit sitting at the kitchen table drinking coffee, a newspaper open in front of him.

"Good morning," he greeted.

"You're here."

"I am."

Praise God, her prayers had been answered. *Don't get ahead of yourself.*

"For how long?" She casually approached him.

"For the duration." Whit closed the newspaper and reached for Mia.

Excitement warred with melancholy. She'd dreamed of a scene like this where she'd come into her kitchen and be greeted by a gentle, loving man.

"What's wrong?" Whit said. "I thought I'd hold Mia."

"Sure, good idea." She handed Mia to her uncle.

This felt like a dream. Only last night he'd essentially said he was done with Carly and Mia, that he was leaving them behind to assist with the investigation.

"I think Harper may want your help determining if anything is missing from Harry's office."

"I didn't go in there much."

"I made scrambled eggs and ham," he said. "Wasn't sure if the baby ate eggs at her age."

"Where'd you get the eggs?"

"I gave Harper a list of a few things last night and his deputy brought it by this morning. Your breakfast is on a plate in the fridge."

Her breakfast. She liked the sound of that. He'd thought about her needs, her hunger.

"I'll make Mia some oatmeal, too," she said.

Mia squealed and flung her hands up, hitting Whit in the nose.

"Whoa, what did I do?" he said.

"Nothing." She smiled. "That's her hungry squeal."

"As opposed to her happy squeal?"

Carly popped the instant oatmeal into the microwave and turned to Whit. "A completely different sound." She pulled the eggs out of the fridge.

"I do," Whit said.

She turned to him. "You do what?"

"Trust you."

She couldn't look away. His eyes, radiating

warmth, pierced through her chest to her heart. Oh, man, she was in trouble.

The microwave beeped. She quickly turned away.

"That's why I'm still here," he said. "Believe it or not, I trust your judgment about family more than my own right now." Mia kicked and squealed again. "Especially when it comes to hungry babies." He made raspberry noises with his lips to entertain her, then lifted her shirt and kissed her tummy. Mia's squeals morphed into giggles, an amazing sound to hear first thing in the morning.

This man, this man who questioned his own ability as a brother, an uncle and a life partner, was so natural with Mia.

And Carly was falling for him.

She turned away from Whit and Mia to make the baby's oatmeal. With restless sleep and the constant threat of danger, it was no wonder Carly was drifting into fantasyland. A strong cup of coffee would help clear the confusion from her brain.

I trust your judgment about family more than my own right now.

He trusted her. Depended on her judgment. She was honored, and a little scared. That was a big responsibility.

Carly put eggs Whit had made in a bowl for Mia and left some on the plate for herself. She sat at the table and reached for the little girl.

"Why don't you eat? I can feed Mia," Whit said. "Can't I?"

"She can actually feed herself eggs, but it might get a little messy." Carly tucked paper towels around the neckline of Mia's shirt. "Ready, baby girl?"

Whit turned her to face the table. Mia's eyes lit up at the sight of scrambled eggs. She scooped a handful, shoved it into her mouth and made a happy humming sound.

"That's good isn't it?" Carly said.

Whit nodded at Carly's plate. "Go ahead. I got this."

Carly forked her own eggs. "You seem—" she hesitated "—better this morning."

"You mean not so guilt-ridden and grouchy?" he said with a wink.

She nodded.

"Yeah, I'm working on that. Sorry," Whit said.

"You don't have to be sorry about how you feel."

Mia squealed and playfully pounded her hands on the table.

"What brought about the change?" Carly asked. "If you don't mind my asking."

"You did." He looked right at her.

And she couldn't move, couldn't breathe.

Whit's ringing phone shattered the tender moment.

"Want me to?" Carly reached for Mia.

"Nah. Could you answer and put it on speaker?" He nodded at the phone on the kitchen table.

She did as he requested, noting the call was from an unknown number.

"Whittaker," he said, helping Mia catch a piece of runaway scrambled egg.

"Brody, Brody help me."

TWELVE

Whit stilled. "Harry?"

Silence.

He stared at his phone, watching the seconds tick by. The caller hadn't hung up. Carly took Mia from him and the baby squawked as if she didn't want to leave Whit's lap.

"Mia," Harry's voice hushed through the line.

"Harry, where are you?" Whit pressed.

"Is Susan...?"

"She's okay," Whit said. "Tell us where you are."

"I'm not sure. They blindfolded us. I could be anywhere, Brody. I'm not even sure I'm in Colorado."

Just then, Detective Harper knocked and entered the coach house. Whit motioned to keep quiet so Whit could hear his brother.

"Harry, why didn't you call sooner?"

"I didn't have a phone. One of the guards left his behind by mistake."

"Why did they take you? What do they want?"

"Take care of Mia, promise me."

"Harry—"

"Promise," he said, his voice firm, desperate.

"I will. I promise," Whit said. "Who's got you?"

"I'm not sure."

"Do they want money?"

"I gave them money. They want more."

"What else is there?"

"They want to destroy me and Susan… Mia."

"Why would anyone want to do that?"

"Brody, I'm sorry." He suddenly sounded so much younger than his thirty-one years.

"Don't apologize, just tell me what's going on."

"I'm sorry that I blew Mom off all the time. Tell her that, okay?"

"You can tell her the next time—"

"I'm sorry I didn't try to make peace with you sooner."

"We'll talk about it when we get you back, little brother. Tell me about the kidnappers."

Silence.

"Harry?"

"If I don't make it—"

"You will make it because your hero big brother is going to save you, got it? Describe everything you can about these guys and where they took you, like distinct smells or sounds. Do the kidnappers have accents? Have they called each other by name?"

Pulse pounding in his ears, Whit was glad Harper was standing beside him listening in.

"No names," Harry said. "We haven't seen their faces. At first they threatened to kill us if we took off the blindfolds. Now they wear clown masks."

"Foreign?"

"American. Maybe… East Coast. The leader said it's our fault he lost everything so now he's going to take everything from us. He's going to make us feel his misery for the rest of our lives. I…" Harry paused. "I can't think of anyone I've wronged like this, Brody."

"Could it be about Susan's fund-raising for Serenity Resort?"

"You…you know about that?"

"I'm not sure what I know, but the feds are looking into her activities and money has been transferred to an offshore account."

"Susan is so trusting. I had just confirmed my suspicions the day we were taken. Hang on, I think someone's coming," he whispered.

"Leave the phone on so I can hear what's happening."

Five seconds passed. Ten. Whit stared at the phone, willing a sound to give them a clue as to where Harry was and who had him.

Mia sighed and Whit realized he'd better mute his side of the call. As he reached over to do so, Mia burst into giggles that should have lit up the room with joy. Instead, dread coursed through

Whit's chest. Did the kidnapper hear the baby, giving away Harry's location?

A crash and male grunts filled the line.

"Help me tie him down!" a man said.

Whit fisted his hand, the skin taut over his knuckles.

The sounds of more struggling echoed through the phone.

Then nothing.

He couldn't rip his gaze from the screen. Seconds ticked by.

"Is this Brody Whittaker?" a male voice said.

Please, God, let me say the right thing.

"It is."

"We're not done—" he paused "—negotiating with your brother. We'll let you know when we are."

"What do you want?" Whit said.

He waited, tension eating away at his gut.

"Goodbye, Detective."

The call ended.

Later that afternoon Carly sat on the floor entertaining Mia with colorful blocks. Although Whit was physically present, he'd been distant since the phone call. Gone was the playful, loving uncle, replaced by a taciturn, tortured man.

Just when Whit started to show tenderness toward Mia, and warmth toward Carly, he'd been shut down by the kidnapper's words.

They still had Whit's brother and planned on keeping him. Frustration and helplessness oozed off Whit's body.

There had to be something she could do.

He'd spent most of the day on the phone or conferring with Harper about the kidnapper's possible identity. They attempted to trace the unknown number that Harry had called from but couldn't narrow down an exact location. It seemed likely that the kidnapper had lost money in the Serenity Resort investment, so authorities focused on identifying investors in order to build a suspect list.

Carly couldn't believe Mrs. B. was involved in criminal activity. It made no sense. The Bremertons were well off financially. There was no need to steal money from other people.

We need it more than they do, Carly's mother used to rationalize. Susan Bremerton was not like that.

Whit hovered by the coach house window, watching the comings and goings of police. She noticed him glance at his phone a few times and she wondered if he was willing his brother to call again.

"Any news on Mrs. B.'s condition?" Carly said.

"No," Whit answered.

"Do they need me to speak to her, maybe bring Mia for a visit?" Carly offered.

"Not at this time."

Short, clipped answers. That's how he'd responded whenever she tried to engage him. *No conversation allowed* was the message.

She didn't think withdrawing into himself was a good plan.

Grabbing little Mia, she walked over to him, knowing that love could ease the pain of most any trauma.

"Could you hold her for a few minutes? I have to use the washroom."

"Uh, okay," he said, although he didn't automatically reach for his niece like he had this morning.

Carly handed him the baby, turned and went into the bathroom. She splashed water on her face and studied her reflection. "How can I help him?" she whispered. She decided to spend a few moments praying, asking the Lord for guidance and the right words to soothe Whit's heart.

Nothing would heal the pain of not knowing if his brother was going to be okay. Maybe, with God's and Mia's help, Whit could find the strength to shoulder this burden without it destroying him from the inside out.

Carly needed to remind him that he was not alone.

She cracked open the door and hesitated as she heard him speaking in a low voice to the baby.

"I'm doing my best, sweet thing, but I know I'm not your dad. That's who you need right now. Everyone's working around the clock to find your papa and bring him home. We're gonna make sure you're safe—me, the police and Carly. It's a good thing you've got Carly in your life. She's a special woman, a real blessing for our family."

Carly closed her eyes and sighed, not only because of the compliment he'd shared with Mia, but also because his voice was back to normal. Yeah, babies had a way of grounding a person.

"Shh. I love you, sweetheart. We'll get him back. I promise."

Carly stepped into the room and saw Whit rocking Mia in his arms. She must be drifting off to sleep.

"Hey," Carly said quietly.

"She's falling asleep." The surprised awe in his voice touched Carly's heart. "In my arms."

Carly smiled. "A great feeling."

He started to offer the baby back to Carly and she shook her head. "The handoff might wake her. Let's put her in her crib."

"I don't know how to do that."

"Come on."

They went into the bedroom and approached the crib.

"Lay her down slowly," Carly coached.

He hesitated at first, and Carly realized he wanted to hold her for a few more seconds. Then he placed her on her back. She squeaked a little.

"Pacifier?" Carly whispered.

He grabbed a pacifier from the corner of the crib and placed it against her lips. They opened and she took it, sucking hard and drifting into a deep sleep.

As they stood there watching Mia, Carly relished the sight of the sleeping baby and let it fill her with joy. She glanced at Whit, whose tense expression had softened. She wasn't sure what compelled her, but she slipped her hand into his and redirected her attention to Mia. She was precious, like this moment in time. Carly would savor it for as long as possible. She'd remember this sense of peace that she and Whit shared as they stood beside the precious child. Even when the case was solved, and Whit was gone from her life, she'd recall this feeling and use it to brighten her spirits when she was low.

Whit squeezed her hand. She looked into his eyes. She could tell he felt the same way, that he, too, treasured this moment.

Someone tapped on the bedroom door and they broke contact as if they were kids who had been caught kissing.

Carly went to the door and opened it wide to Detective Harper. She placed a finger to her lips. She and Whit joined Harper in the living room.

"You have news about my brother?" Whit said.

"Not yet, sorry. Carly, could you come to the house and check out the office to see if anything obvious is missing?"

"Sure, although I didn't go in there much." She glanced at Whit. "I'll be right back."

* * *

Two hours later, Whit found himself restlessly pacing the living room.

He wanted Carly to return, and not because she needed to care for Mia. The baby was still asleep. No, Whit missed Carly's calming presence. Whenever she was around, he could almost feel that elusive sense of peace, like when they'd been standing over the crib.

And she took his hand.

When she touched him, the incessant angst seemed to dissolve a bit, drifting away from his body. How was that possible? How could the touch of one person have that kind of effect on him? He also liked having her close because she helped him stay grounded and keep his perspective, which he needed to find his way out of his own misery to help his brother.

Take care of Mia, promise me.

Of course he'd take care of his niece, no matter how long Harry was gone, even if the worst happened—Susan was sent to prison, and they weren't able to rescue Harry.

Only now did Whit realize how much he would need Carly to make that happen, to help him be a stable, loving uncle. Together Whit and Carly could give Mia what she needed, but without Carly?

Whit wasn't sure how he'd manage.

Whoa, you sound like a man in love.

Not possible. He'd known Carly only a few days, and she came with plenty of her own baggage, including a juvenile arrest and complicated family.

None of which would matter if you loved her.

He thought he'd loved Pamela, his longtime girlfriend, but in the end that didn't work out. At the beginning of their romance, he'd liked how much she relied on him. In retrospect that relationship supported his "hero" mode. Having someone look up to him, rely on his knowledge and emotional strength, was great for his ego and made him feel like he was doing something good for another person. He always assumed that love meant taking care of someone else first and foremost.

When he couldn't find the courage to propose after two years of dating, he questioned what was holding him back. Initially he thought it was the kid thing—she wanted kids and he didn't—and then he blamed it on his commitment to the job.

Spending time with Carly raised another possibility. Whit needed someone as strong as he was who could offer peace and balance. Someone fearless.

Like Carly.

Even if Whit hadn't come to her rescue at the river, he knew Carly would have protected the baby from the kidnappers. She was smart and incredibly determined. She'd been through plenty yet hadn't given up on herself, in part thanks to her faith, something Whit felt he was missing in his life and didn't know how to access.

He remembered her praying in the car and then opening her striking hazel eyes. *See? It's that easy.*

Whit took a deep breath and for the second time he prayed. "Please, God, take care of my brother. Don't let me lose him this way, not before we can make things right. Amen."

The tightness in his chest eased a bit and hope sparked to life.

The sound of a baby crying drew his attention to the bedroom. Mia had awakened and probably needed a diaper change.

"This oughta be interesting," he muttered. It was only the second time he'd done this, and the first time he had help from the innkeeper. How would Mia react to Whit showing up without Carly by his side? He went to the crib and picked her up. "Hey, baby girl. You have a good sleep?"

She whined in response. He had to admit she was a great kid, especially considering the upheaval of the past few days.

"I'll bet you need a change."

She rubbed her eyes and the whining intensified. Carly had set up a makeshift changing table on the dresser and he'd seen her change the baby's diaper a few times.

"Let's see if I do this as well as your aunt Carly."

Aunt Carly. It felt natural to call her that. She

seemed like a part of the family, much more than a nanny at this point, and he assumed she'd always be a special person in Mia's life, even after this case was solved and they got Harry back.

He laid Mia on the dresser and pulled off her pants. She kicked her feet, obviously happy that she was getting the drenched diaper off her bottom.

The wipes, powder and fresh diaper were within reach, so Whit got to work. A minute later he was quite proud of himself after having successfully changed the diaper. Maybe he didn't need Carly after all.

Uh, wrong. He needed Carly…for more than diaper changes.

"Need help?" Carly said from the doorway.

"Actually, I think I got it." He looked up and noted her strained expression, arms hugging her midsection. "What's wrong?"

"Other than you have powder on your…" With a half smile, she pointed at his shirt.

He glanced down. Splotches of white baby powder covered his black cotton shirt. "And here I was so proud of myself."

As he held Mia, Carly checked the diaper job. "Hey, that's pretty good."

"You're not so good, are you?" he asked.

She wandered into the living room and he followed, carrying Mia.

"You were gone a long time," Whit said.

She nodded, slowly sitting at the table.

"What is it?" he prompted.

"The intruder broke into your brother's safe and, Harper suspects, stole documents."

"And...?" He waited.

"There were other things in the safe, things they left behind, like a private investigator's report about me and my parents. Your brother hired a private detective to dig into my past. He also discovered my parents were serving time. No information about Greta, though."

"Is that what's upsetting you? That your parents are in jail?"

"No, they made their choices and I've moved on from my past. What upsets me is that he hired someone to check on my story. If he was that worried, why bother hiring me in the first place?"

"He was being thorough. Put yourself in his shoes. As a father, he was welcoming you into his home to take care of the most precious thing in his life. He needed to be sure he could trust you."

"I thought he trusted me when I explained my background."

"Some of us do better with proof."

"Yeah, well, it's frustrating when your word is never good enough."

"I'm sure your word is good enough for him now," he said. "I know it's good enough for me."

She glanced up. "Thanks."

Sadness welled in her eyes. Whit wanted to hold her, tell her everything was going to be okay.

He passed her the baby. Holding Mia seemed to snap Whit out of whatever anguish he was struggling with, so he hoped it would do the same for Carly.

Carly smiled. "Baby love is exactly what I need."

A firm knock echoed across the room. Whit opened the door to Detective Harper.

"We've got a lead on your brother's location," Harper said.

"Let me get my coat," Whit said.

"Whoa, you're not going anywhere."

Right, Whit was an uncle and a brother first; a cop second.

"I'm letting you know because I'll need as many men as I can spare, which means—"

"Take them all. I'll protect Carly and the baby."

"You sure? Because I could leave a deputy—"

"No, I got this."

"I'll let you know as soon as we find something." Harper left.

Whit and Carly waited for what seemed like hours to hear back from Detective Harper, but only ten minutes had passed. Whit was growing more anxious by the minute.

"It's great that they have a solid lead," Carly said, bouncing Mia on her lap.

"It certainly is." They'd found his brother. Maybe. Possibly.

Please, God, let them find my brother and bring him home.

A ringing phone interrupted his silent prayer.

"Oh, that's mine," Carly said, leaning Mia against her shoulder while digging the phone out of her pocket.

"Here, I can hold her," Whit offered.

"No, I'm good." Carly placed the phone on the table. The caller ID read Sam. "It's Mia's biological mother."

Whit pressed the speaker button.

"Hello?" Carly said.

"He found you. You've gotta go!"

"Who found us?" Carly said.

"Sam, this is Brody Whittaker, Mia's uncle." Silence.

"Sam, he's on our side," Carly tried.

"He's a cop," she responded in a low voice.

"I'm also Mia's uncle and would do anything to protect her. Who found us?"

"You've gotta get out of there!"

"We shouldn't leave the compound," Whit said.

"His men are probably on the way. The police left, right? That was him, luring them away from the house."

"But we're safe here," Carly said. "The access codes have been changed."

"They have a program that will break the code."

"How do you know that?" Whit said.

"Because I wrote it. Meet me at Freeland State Park in an hour, just the three of you, and I'll explain everything."

"Better idea, why don't you meet us at the Summit County Sheriff's Office," Whit said.

"Why can't you believe me? Oh, no! They're at the front gate. Use the back driveway and stay out of sight near the exit. I'll open the gates and let them in, then you drive out of there and I'll close the gates behind you. Go!"

Carly stood, clutching Mia against her chest. Whit checked his phone, which he'd synced to the home surveillance system. Sure enough, an SUV with two men was parked at the front gate. The driver was punching in codes.

"Get Mia's things," Whit said to Carly. "How did they know we were here?" Whit asked the mystery woman on the phone.

"I'll explain later. Meet me at the picnic area just outside Freeland State Park. One hour. Don't let anything happen to Mia."

Whit's instincts told him Sam wasn't messing with him, that she genuinely cared about Mia's safety. Plus, Carly vouched for her, which held weight in Whit's book.

They did as Sam suggested and, headlights off, used the back driveway to approach the front gate. Whit parked and they stayed low as they waited.

"I hope this isn't a setup," he muttered.

"Have a little faith," Carly said.

"I'm tryin'."

"Sam texted me. I told her we're in position. She's opening the gates."

Neither of them could see what was going on, both because they were partially blocked by the shrubbery, and because they were hunkered down. Whit eyed his phone and watched a black SUV speed through the open gate.

"Now?" he said.

"Wait," Carly said.

Buckled in the car seat, Mia squeaked and kicked her feet.

"Someone's ready to get outta here," Whit said.

"Okay, go!"

Whit turned over the engine and shoved it into gear.

He didn't want to peel out and draw attention, so he slowly pressed the accelerator.

The gates started to close.

"What's she doing?" Whit said. "We're not through!"

THIRTEEN

"They must be closing automatically," Carly said. "That's normal."

"I thought she said she could control them."

He gripped the steering wheel. Easy targets. If the intruders figured out they'd fled the coach house, they'd double back and find them sitting here, waiting to be picked off.

The gates closed completely.

"Carly," he said.

"Hang on, she's not responding."

"This feels like a setup."

"Don't say that."

He glanced out the side window. Couldn't quite see the coach house. Two guys. He knew two guys had breached the property.

"I'm out of moves here," Whit said. Calling the police wouldn't do him any good. It would take too long for them to respond. "Anything?"

"Come on, come on," Carly muttered.

Whit took a deep breath, then another. Counted

to five. The perps must have figured out that Carly and Whit had fled with the baby.

He scanned the property for another option. Any other option.

There was none. They were trapped in a cage with their enemy.

"I'm calling 9-1-1."

"Okay, she's got it," Carly said.

The gates slowly opened.

He could sense the guys coming after him, speeding up the drive.

No, change your focus. Focus on getting away and protecting the people you care about: Mia and Carly.

He'd made a promise to his brother and intended to keep it.

In those last few seconds it took for the gates to open, he realized he'd also made a promise to himself: when this case was over, and they were out of danger, he would not only mend his relationship with Harry, but would also pursue a relationship with Carly.

There was something there, something bigger and more powerful than he'd ever felt with another woman.

What a crazy thing to be thinking about right now.

The gates were nearly open…

Flickering headlights drew his attention to his rearview mirror.

"Stay down!" he ordered Carly.

He'd never make it through and leave the perps behind. Not at the speed they were going.

"New plan. Get behind the wheel," he said.

"What?"

"I need you to drive away when the gates fully open."

"I'm not leaving you."

"Yes you will. For Mia's sake."

He scrambled out of the car and found cover twenty feet away. Best-case scenario: he'd immobilize their vehicle. Worst case, he'd draw their fire and be shot. Either way, it would give Carly a chance to escape with Mia.

As he hid beside a tree, he ignored the muscle injury that was supposed to prevent him from successfully using his right arm to fire a weapon.

The gates were fully open.

Whit motioned for Carly to get away.

He turned toward the assailants.

Aimed low…

Took a breath.

Fired off three shots. At least one of them hit the SUV's tire and sent it careening into a tree.

Whit took off after Carly. He wasn't sure how long he had before the perps extricated themselves and started shooting. Whit did not want them shooting at the car. He waved his arm for her to keep going.

Carly drove safely away. The gates started to close.

Whit ran faster, his gaze fixated on the sedan he'd bought in Cold Creek Springs. It disappeared around the corner. Out of sight.

"There!" a man shouted behind him.

The gates squeaked as they continued to ease shut.

He slid through a gap sideways, tore off down the private road and spotted brake lights. Carly was waiting for him.

The clunk of locking gates echoed behind him. Good, they were safe.

A gunshot rang out. Whit automatically ducked and yanked the car door open. "Go, go, go!"

Mia was crying. Carly was as white as a sheet as she clung to the steering wheel and sped away from the mansion toward the interstate.

When Whit asked Carly to pull over and offered to drive, she didn't argue. Her hands still trembled from the trauma of being shot at. Besides, she needed to climb into the back seat and comfort Mia.

She parked on the side of the road. As she and Whit changed spots and crossed in front of the car, Whit unexpectedly pulled her into a hug, an embrace that warmed some of the fear right out of her body.

"We're okay," he said, and then released her.

With renewed confidence that they were safe, at least for the moment, Carly slid into the back seat beside Mia. She wiped tears off the little girl's cheeks and popped the binky into her mouth.

Humming softly to calm both herself and Mia, Carly thanked God for their swift escape.

"You shouldn't have waited," Whit said suddenly.

"Excuse me?"

"You should have driven off with the baby."

"And leave you to be killed?"

"The baby has to be the priority, Carly." He caught her eye in the rearview. "Can we agree on that?"

"Whit—"

"If there's a choice between Mia and me, you've got to choose Mia. I can defend myself. The baby is completely vulnerable."

Carly sighed and eyed Mia's reddened cheeks. Although Whit was right, Carly couldn't have abandoned him. Were her feelings for Whit putting Mia in jeopardy?

She thought about that for a second. No, she'd calculated the risk and knew Whit could make it out through the gates, that he'd follow the car and would join them around the corner.

"I understand what you're saying," she started. "But I knew you'd get out of there safely."

"Not if I'd been shot."

The thought sent a shiver across her shoulders. "You weren't shot."

"They were shooting at us through the gates. What if they'd hit the car?"

"They couldn't hit the car from that angle."

"You don't know that, unless you've become a forensics expert in the past few days."

She didn't appreciate his biting comment or his snappy tone, although she sensed it came from a place of worry about losing his niece. He already might have lost his brother, and to lose his niece, as well? Brody Whittaker was a strong man, but that would devastate him.

"You're right. I'm sorry," she said.

"Aw, Carly, I don't want you to apologize. I want you guys to be safe."

"I know. I'm—"

"Don't say you're sorry."

"I was going to say I'm grateful for your concern, truly."

"I'll call Harper," he said, indicating the end to their conversation.

He put his phone on the dash and hesitated before making the call.

"If anything happened to you guys…"

She reached across the front seat and placed her hand on his shoulder. "I know."

He called the detective and it went into his voice mail.

"It's Whittaker. The property was breached. We escaped and left the assailants locked inside the compound. We're on our way to a rendezvous with Mia's biological mother. She claims to have information about what's going on. We'll be at—"

"Whit," Carly interrupted. "She wants to meet us alone."

"I won't risk it. Harper, if you get this message, we'll be at Freeland State Park in an hour."

Carly leaned back against the seat, frustrated. Sam asked to meet the three of them, no cops. What would she do if police showed up? Then again, they were busy following the lead on Mr. Bremerton's whereabouts.

A lead that might be a distraction devised by whomever was after the baby. Sam's words suddenly resonated with Carly.

The police left, right? That was probably him, luring them away from the house.

Oh, man. Carly hoped that wasn't the case. She hoped Harper and his deputies were following up on a legitimate lead. She wondered if Sam's comment had sunk in with Whit, but decided not to ask.

"Tell me again why you think we should trust this Sam person," Whit said.

"She's Mia's mother."

"Maybe all this is about getting her baby back."

"She said she wasn't good with kids and pleaded with me to take care of Mia. She wants what's best for the baby."

"You can't know that for sure."

"You didn't see her eyes."

"I hope you're right, Carly, I do, but you can see why I think it's a good idea to have backup."

"I wish it wasn't the police. She doesn't like the police."

"That's a red flag right there."

"Not necessarily. I don't like cops either, remember? And I'd give my life to protect Mia."

When he didn't respond, Carly thought she might have won her argument, even though a small part of her agreed with him that backup would be wise in this situation. What if the bad guys were tracking Sam? Then again, Sam seemed like a smart woman, especially considering she'd controlled the gates at the Bremerton home.

Sam obviously didn't like cops and Carly figured it was due to questionable tech activity. Carly had learned as a young adult that you couldn't keep running from your mistakes; you had to face them head-on. Otherwise they kept coming at you in different ways, until you finally learned the lesson.

Which, in Carly's case, tended to be the lesson of self-forgiveness.

Mia squealed and kicked her feet.

"What's going on back there?" Whit said.

"She's probably hungry."

"Do you have any food?"

"Not much in the diaper bag. A few crackers I think."

"Let's pick something up on the way to the park."

"You sure we can risk it?"

"I'll go shopping and you stay in the car with Mia. This time if there's trouble, you take off, got it?"

"Yes, sir." She saluted.

"I'm serious."

"I know. Sorry."

Carly had to try to lighten the mood. She didn't like thinking about leaving Whit behind, much less talking about it. On some level she knew he was right, that Mia's safety had to come first.

She prayed that she'd never be put in the position of having to make the choice between the two of them.

Whit parked at an outlook where he could see the entrance to the state park. He and Carly ate sandwiches while he kept an eye on the picnic area in the distance.

He'd texted Harper with his location. The detective hadn't responded. Whit hoped Harper couldn't return text messages because he was in the midst of finding Harry.

"Such a good girl," Carly said in the back seat.

"How's she doing?" Whit asked.

"She's loving her carrots, aren't ya, baby girl?"

"How about you, you get anything to eat?"

"I'll finish my sandwich in a minute."

"I'll come back there and feed her so you can eat."

Whit got into the back seat on the other side of Mia and took over feeding duty.

"Thanks." Carly picked up her sandwich. "Can I ask you something?"

"Sure." He held another spoon of mushy baby food to Mia's lips. She opened them and her eyes lit up.

"Why are you on a leave of absence?" Carly asked.

He didn't answer at first, not sure how much to tell her.

"Sorry, too intrusive?"

"Nah. I was injured and they haven't given me medical clearance to return to work."

"Still suffering from the injuries?" She bit into her sandwich.

"Yep. Still struggling with headaches, occasional dizziness, plus they weren't sure my arm would heal properly so I may not be able to shoot accurately."

"But you shot the bad guys' tires at the house."

"True."

"Okay, here's another question, why police work?"

"Why a nurse?"

"I asked you first."

"You'll laugh."

"I promise I won't."

"I like helping people. You'd be surprised how many of us get into this line of work for that very reason. To help people, to do good work in the community."

"Huh," she said softly.

"You had a bad experience with cops so you assume all cops are jerks. There are bad people in every line of work, not just police work."

"Bad cops have more of a negative impact."

"Do they? What about bad nurses or doctors? When people go the hospital, they're extremely vulnerable. What if they encounter a rude or insensitive medical professional? How do you think that makes them feel?"

"Pretty bad, actually."

"You can't paint the entire police force with the same brush, Carly. I mean look at me. I'm not a jerk, am I?"

"Mostly not."

"Mostly, huh?" He smiled and wiped food off Mia's cheek.

"You're not a jerk," she said. "You're...unusual."

"Unusual?"

"I don't mean that in a bad way."

"Uh-huh."

"I meant, I haven't met many guys who have

the strength of character that you do along with a gentle side."

He nodded at Mia. "I think this little charmer brings out that side of me."

"You ever think about having children?"

"Gotta get married first, and I haven't found anyone willing to put up with my long hours or cocky attitude."

"You've never dated?"

"Sure, I've dated." He stopped for a second, not wanting to share the details about his relationship with Pamela. Then he remembered whom he was talking to. "Even had a serious girlfriend for a couple of years."

"What happened?"

"Didn't work out."

"Long hours and cocky attitude?"

"Something like that."

"Too bad. You'd be a great father."

"What about you?" he said, uncomfortable with her comment. "Surely you've had a serious relationship or two."

A part of him hoped she hadn't. Again, selfish.

"No time for romance, what with working full-time and going to school. I do want children some-day. Taking care of Mia has opened my heart to that possibility."

"You weren't sure before taking care of Mia if you wanted kids?"

"I didn't think I'd be a good mom, considering I wasn't able to save Greta."

"Stop doing that."

"What?"

"Blaming yourself for something you couldn't control when you were a kid. It wasn't your job to protect your sister. It was your parents' job."

"Yeah, well, that wasn't happening. And I failed."

"Careful. You're starting to sound like a hypocrite."

"Excuse me?"

"You talk about how God forgives, yet you can't forgive yourself. Aren't you supposed to follow God's lead?"

"Of course, but—"

"Then let it go. If God has forgiven you, it's time you forgive yourself."

She frowned and studied her sandwich.

Way to offend her, Whit. Now she's giving you the silent treatment.

He wiped food off Mia's cheeks. "It's almost time." He glanced out the window and didn't see anyone at the picnic area. A part of him wanted to stay put and wait until Sam showed up before he exposed himself, Carly and Mia, or even wait for backup.

As he opened the door, he felt Carly's hand on his arm. He glanced at her.

"Thanks," she said.

"For what?"

"For calling me out. You're right. I have been carrying this burden way too long."

"You were a kid, Carly."

"So were you."

"What do you mean?"

"When your brother got hurt."

"That's different."

"Because…?"

"I was older, seventeen, arrogant and self-centered. Some would say I haven't changed much."

"Not me. I see a man wanting to heal his family, save his brother and protect his niece. That's not self-centered at all."

Somehow, through her eyes, Whit saw a different side of himself, a side he didn't think existed. In a flash, it opened up myriad possibilities for the future.

The possibilities were quickly crushed when the self-critical voice echoed through his brain: *You'd be a bad husband and a horrible father.*

"What happened?" Carly said.

He cocked his head.

"You seemed good for a second, then your expression changed."

How was it possible that she could read him so easily?

"Let's concentrate on our meeting with Sam." He exited the car and hesitated half a second before getting behind the wheel. He couldn't afford to be distracted by the possibility of living a different life, a better life with a woman like Carly. Those thoughts were dangerous on many levels. He had to stay alert and determined to protect the passengers in his back seat.

A beep indicated a text message. He got into the car and checked his phone. "Harper is on the way."

"Let's get over there and talk to her before the cops scare her off."

He eyed the picnic area. Still no Sam.

His own instinct seemed to be inaccessible, not giving him a clear signal as to the right course of action.

"Ready?" she said.

Whether it was the concussion or lack of a solid night's sleep, Whit was off-kilter. Once again, he relied on Carly's judgment to make a decision. He put the car in gear and headed for the picnic area. Eyes darting to the rearview, side mirrors and up ahead, he kept constant surveillance on his surroundings.

Everything was clear. There were no cars in the immediate area, and police backup was on the way.

He turned onto the road leading to the state park, the picnic area up ahead.

Mia cooed in the back seat, obviously happy about having a full tummy. The sound made him smile.

You'd be a great father.

Would he? Was he being a good father by driving his niece into a potentially dangerous situation?

"Over there!" Carly said, pointing out the front window.

He spotted a young woman in the distance, stumbling out of the woods to a picnic table. She collapsed, looking either exhausted from hiking, or drunk.

Whit did another scan of the area. The park ranger office was up ahead, blinds closed. He parked the car.

"You and the baby stay here," he said.

"She doesn't know you."

Before he could open his mouth to argue, Carly was out the door. She wasn't far away, maybe only thirty feet. He wanted to go after her, bring her back to the car where she'd be safe.

A squeak from the back seat reminded him why he needed to stay put.

Eyes darting from the rearview mirror to the scene unfolding in front of him, he took a deep breath, ready for anything.

He watched as Carly sat next to Sam, who was hunched over, looking at something. Her phone?

Carly put her arm around Sam.

Suddenly Sam shoved Carly off the bench seat.

Whit gripped the door handle. Eyed Mia through the rearview. Looked back out front.

With a surprised expression, Carly stood up and held out her hands.

They were covered in blood.

FOURTEEN

Whit flung open the door.

"It's not my blood!" Carly called out to him. "Stay there!"

Heart pounding, he struggled to tamp down the anguish ripping through his chest. For a second when he thought Carly had been wounded…

He'd never felt anything like that before, and he'd seen his share of blood in his line of work. He wanted her to get back to the car. ASAP.

If it wasn't her blood it was Sam's, which meant the kidnappers had found her and they could be close.

"Get back to the car!" he called out.

She seemed to be negotiating with Sam. Carly grabbed Sam's arm, pulled her off the picnic bench and helped her to the car. From this vantage point, Whit saw blood staining Sam's jacket sleeve.

With a clenched jaw, Carly practically carried

Sam to the vehicle, and Whit took over as they got close.

"Put her in front," Carly said.

He helped Sam into the front seat and shut the door.

Carly climbed into the back with Mia and they took off, Sam clutching her arm to her stomach.

"Hospital," Carly said.

"No, they'll find me," Sam protested.

"They already found you, and you need medical attention," Carly argued. "She's got a deep laceration on her arm," she explained to Whit.

Mia started whimpering, probably picking up on the anxious energy in the car.

"It's okay, sweetie," Carly soothed.

"I'll call Harper." Whit reached for his phone on the dash holder, but Sam grabbed it first.

"Who's Harper?" she asked.

"The detective trying to find my brother."

"No cops. No hospital." She shoved the phone in her pocket.

Carly reached into the front seat and placed a hand on Sam's shoulder. "You care about your daughter, right?"

"Of course I do."

"What are we going to tell her when she wants to meet her biological mother? That we let her mom bleed to death because she was a stubborn Sally? Is that what we should tell her?"

Sam turned to look at Mia. "She won't want to meet me. I abandoned her."

"Stop thinking about yourself, Sam," Carly said. "You can't die on this little girl."

"She has a mama and a papa."

"Well, her mother might be going to jail and her father is still missing. Step up and be a good parent."

Whit was surprised by Carly's assertive tone, and appreciated it. Her challenge seemed to snap Sam out of her downward spiral.

"Okay, take me to the hospital." She sighed. "But if he finds me again...he will kill me."

"My phone," Whit said.

"When we get to the hospital," Sam said.

"Who did this to you?" Whit asked.

"A guy hired by Mia's biological father."

"Tell Whit what you told me about the kidnappers," Carly encouraged.

"Mia's father," Sam started. "He's a brutal man."

"I thought this was about my sister-in-law's fund-raising activity," Whit said.

"No, it's Levi."

"Levi?" Whit said.

"Levi Moore. His family is into racketeering back east. I... I didn't know that when they hired me to do IT work. Levi was—" she hesitated "—charming. I fell in love with him."

"Levi's got my brother?"

"Yes. I'm sorry, it's my fault."

"What do you mean?"

"I said I didn't know who the father was, but Mia is Levi's child. I was pregnant when I found out the truth about his family. I disappeared, went off the grid. I couldn't let my baby be raised by criminals. I wanted her to have a nice home and loving parents. I moved to Colorado and answered an ad for a private adoption."

"Levi knew about your pregnancy?" Whit asked.

"Yes. We were planning our wedding when I found out the truth and left. I was four months pregnant."

"You could have gone to the feds," Whit said.

"I didn't want to be arrested for helping the Moore family, even though I didn't, not intentionally anyway."

"The feds would have taken that into consideration."

"If you say so." She hesitated. "I guess I should apologize about before, at the house."

"You mean the gates?" Whit said.

"No. I was the one who broke into the Bremerton house. I needed to check his computer, see if there was any communication between Mr. Bremerton and Levi, using an alias. I was trying to confirm my suspicions. I'd hoped I was wrong." Sam smiled weakly at Mia. "She is so beautiful."

"And sweet. The perfect little girl," Carly said.

"I should have known Levi would never give

up looking for us. Please, don't let anything happen to her."

"We won't," Whit said.

Sam sighed and closed her eyes.

The hospital ER was a buzz of activity. Carly and Whit sat in the waiting area with Mia on her lap. Whit constantly scanned their surroundings.

Mia's criminal father wouldn't send henchmen into a public hospital, would he? According to Sam, he was capable of much worse.

Things were looking grim for the Bremerton family, especially since Mia's biological father was determined to get his child back by any means necessary.

"Harper is on the way," Whit said to Carly. "Plus, they assigned a deputy to Sam, and one by the front entrance to the hospital."

He must have guessed what she'd been thinking.

"Did they find your brother?"

"No, they got there too late."

"You mean—"

"They got away."

She sighed with relief that they hadn't found Mr. B.'s dead body.

"There was evidence Harry had been there," Whit said. "Harper's bringing it with him."

"I'm sorry," she said.

"He's still alive. I know he's still alive."

"Should we talk to Mrs. Bremerton? Maybe she—"

"She's been uncommunicative since yesterday."

"Surely the baby can bring her around."

"The baby can't fix everything, Carly," he said, rather sharply.

He was frustrated and no doubt worried sick. She decided to leave it alone and refocus on Mia. The child had been through so much this week.

Detective Harper turned the corner and joined them. "Does this look familiar?" He offered Whit an evidence bag with a medallion hanging from a silver chain.

Whit nodded. "It was mine. I put it in Harry's room when I left for boot camp. I… I didn't know he still had it."

The vacant expression on his face made Carly want to hug him, warm his cheek with her palm, hand him the baby.

But Whit was right. The innocence of a child couldn't fix everything and wouldn't wash the pain away.

He stood suddenly and paced. She studied Mia's little fingers as they clung to a teething ring. If Whit turned and Carly saw tears in his eyes…

It would break her heart, and this wasn't the time or place for that kind of intense emotion.

She needed to be strong.

"What's next?" she asked Detective Harper.

"I'll interview the biological mother and see if

she has anything we can use to find the kidnappers. I've been in touch with the feds. The Moore family has been under surveillance and is close to being charged with multiple counts of racketeering. It's just a matter of time—"

"Which we don't have," Whit said. "We need to find my brother and soon."

"We're working on it—24/7."

"And the feds?"

"We're working with them, as well. In the meantime, we need to get you to a safe house."

"Sam is worried that Levi Moore will find her in the hospital and kill her," Carly said.

"Which is why we've assigned a deputy to her."

Whit's phone rang, and an odd expression creased his brow.

"What is it?" Carly said.

"I'll be right back." He walked away.

She watched him pause down the hall, intent on his conversation.

"How are you holding up?" the detective asked.

She glanced at Detective Harper. She'd almost forgotten he was there. "Okay I guess. I'm worried about Mr. Bremerton."

"If he's tough like his brother, he'll be okay. I'm starting to think this is about revenge, not simple murder."

"Well, that's comforting," Carly said in a sarcastic tone. She strained to see down the hall. Whit had disappeared.

* * *

Whit gripped the phone. Had to keep it together.

"I'm done with your brother," a man's voice said. "You can come pick him up."

"Is he...?" Whit had to ask.

"He's still breathing. For now."

"If you hurt him—"

"I'm in charge here, Whittaker. Follow my instructions and you'll see your brother again, alive. If you involve the cops, well..."

Whit waited. "What?"

"Cops equals corpse. It's that simple. And bring my daughter. We've been apart far too long."

If Whit refused, Harry was dead. Yet Whit had no intention of handing Mia over to this monster.

"Ten p.m. Willows Landing."

"Let me talk to my brother."

A few seconds of silence passed, then a hoarse voice said, "Brody...?"

"Harry, are you okay?"

"I'm... Mia?"

"She's fine, she's—"

"That's enough," Levi said. "Don't be late, Detective."

The call ended. Whit sighed with frustration. He had less than two hours to figure this out. If he didn't bring Mia, the guy would kill his brother. If he did bring her...

He'd promised his brother to protect Mia at all costs.

But he couldn't let Harry die.

"Whit?"

He turned to see Carly and the detective walking toward him. Mia waved her arms and reached for Whit.

Carly tried to redirect the baby's attention to a toy, but Mia seemed intent on getting attention from Whit. He took her and gave her a loving hug.

"I'm sorry, sweetie," he whispered against her ear, because his decision meant she'd grow up fatherless, and Whit would lose a brother.

"What's going on?" Carly said.

He finally looked at her, and then Detective Harper. "Levi Moore called. I'm supposed to meet him at 10:00 p.m. with the baby."

"Whit—"

"I agreed in order to buy time," he interrupted Carly. "He said if I involve cops, my brother is dead."

"If you don't, he'll kill you and take the child," Harper countered.

"What do we do?" Carly asked.

"First, we get you to a safe house," Harper said. "Come on." He motioned them down the hall to the stairwell. Harper called one of his deputies and gave him instructions to meet downstairs.

Whit clung to Mia, blowing raspberries against her cheek to make her giggle. There was no way he was going to surrender this precious child and he couldn't sacrifice his brother either.

When they reached the side exit to the hospital, an unmarked car was waiting. They quickly got in back.

"Where's the car seat?" Carly said.

"No time. It's not that far," Harper said. "Deputy Schneider will get you to the safe house. I'll come by shortly and we'll make a plan for the meet-up." Harper tapped the top of the car and stepped back.

Deputy Schneider pulled away a little too fast.

"Slow down, we've got a baby in the back seat," Whit said.

"Sorry, sorry," the deputy said.

As Carly stroked Mia's hair, Whit said, "He's still alive. I spoke to my brother."

"That's great news," she said.

"I don't know what to do. Either way I lose."

"Don't talk like that. We'll figure something out."

The car suddenly sped up.

"Deputy—"

"I think someone's following us," Schneider said.

Whit glanced out the back window and was blinded by piercing headlights.

"They're too close," Carly said.

"Call it in," Whit ordered.

The deputy grabbed the radio. "Dispatch, I need backup, someone's—"

They were suddenly jerked forward.

"Whit!" Carly shouted.

"Hold on!"

Whit clung to Mia, his arms stronger than any car seat.

It couldn't end like this. He'd made a promise to his brother.

And he loved Carly.

They were hit again and the baby squealed as the car spun out of control.

FIFTEEN

Carly slammed back against the seat. Mia burst into tears.

Whit handed Mia to Carly. "Stay in the car and keep the doors locked."

"What are you—"

He was gone before she could finish her sentence. The car had swerved off the road, headlong into a tree.

"It's okay, sweetie." Carly patted Mia's back to soothe her, while trying to control her own frazzled nerves. She strained to see out the back window.

Tapping against the glass made her shriek. A man motioned to her from the other side of the window. "Open the door!"

She wouldn't surrender that easily. Whit ordered her to stay in the car. Police backup had to be on the way, right?

"I said open!"

She decided to pretend he wasn't there. He tapped again, this time with his gun.

Whit sprung out of nowhere, tackling the guy to the ground. Carly clung to Mia and prayed.

A second guy dived into the fight. Whit was outnumbered.

She had to do something.

"Deputy!" she shouted at Deputy Schneider, who'd been consumed by the airbag.

Whit was on the ground and being kicked repeatedly by the two men.

One of the guys stopped kicking, stepped up to the window and pointed the gun at Carly. Carly flung open the door, nearly hitting him in the gut.

"Are you an idiot?" she said. "You're going to shoot us? What do you think your boss will say about that, about shooting his daughter?"

The guy took a step back and looked at her like she was insane. Well, that's how she felt right now—crazy enough to lay down her life for the two people she loved: the child in her arms and the man on the ground. She cast a quick glance at Whit who seemed semiconscious. She hoped his head wasn't injured again.

Girl, you've got bigger problems than Whit's concussion.

"His boss would be most displeased," a voice said.

She glanced at the SUV behind them. A broad-shouldered man in his forties sauntered toward her. He had dark, empty eyes and a cold expression. This had to be Levi Moore.

Her grip tightened on Mia.

"So this is my child," he said, reaching out to touch the back of Mia's head. The little girl hadn't stopped crying. "Daddy's here." His voice made Carly nauseous. He motioned for one of his men to take Mia.

"Not happening." Carly backed up and formulated a plan to ingratiate herself to the criminal.

Levi raised an assessing eyebrow.

"Mia doesn't know you and she's already upset," Carly started. "If you truly care about her, you'll put her needs first. Do you know anything about babies?"

Levi narrowed his eyes.

"I do," Carly continued. "I'm her nanny and I'm studying to be a nurse. I've raised this child since she was four weeks old. You need me."

"Do I?" he said.

She ignored the shudder trickling down her spine. *Don't stop now.*

"Yes. I can keep her happy and healthy. Where she goes, I go."

"Give me the kid," one of the thugs said, aiming a gun at Carly.

She didn't flinch. She'd already committed herself to dying to protect Mia.

"Put that away," Levi ordered, then addressed Carly. "You'd die to protect my child?"

"Of course. I love her like she's my own. I've been the one constant in her life. Susan Bremerton didn't love her like I do. She was rarely home. She didn't sing to her at night before bed or sit on the floor and play blocks. She doesn't know Mia's favorite food or how she likes her belly rubbed. It's been all me for the past six months. I don't care who's paying my salary as long as I can take care of Mia. She needs me."

"Boss, we gotta go," one of his men said.

Levi held her gaze. Carly broke eye contact only to place a pacifier in Mia's mouth to help soothe her.

He motioned Carly toward the SUV. "We'll negotiate terms later."

"Wait." She crouched and grabbed Whit's phone. "We don't want him calling for help."

She pocketed the phone and went to the SUV. She hoped she could discreetly turn on the location services so Whit could use it to find her.

"What about him?" one of the guys said.

"Kill him."

Carly spun around. "No, don't!"

Levi studied her.

"Killing a cop will put a bull's-eye on our back and make it impossible to get out of town. Local cops will rally to find us. Are you going to risk putting your daughter in that kind of danger, getting hit by a stray bullet?"

Levi smiled and put out his hand to stop his men from killing Whit.

He leaned closer to Carly. "I like your style. Shall we?" He motioned her to the car.

She did it. She'd convinced Levi not to kill Whit. Relief settled across her shoulders.

Although what came next, she had no idea. She hoped, she prayed, that Whit would figure out what she was up to and come find her, wherever she ended up.

Whit groaned and got to his knees. A hissing sound echoed behind him from the unmarked patrol car. He struggled to stand, gripping bruised ribs that screeched in pain.

Not nearly as loud as his own guilt. Whit allowed Carly and Mia to be taken by Levi Moore. Now that Levi had his child, there was less motivation for him to return Harry alive.

Whit dug in his pocket for his phone and remembered Carly taking it. *We don't want him calling for help.*

Could he have been so wrong about her, so drawn in by her gentle charm and sincere eyes that he'd missed what she truly was?

Let it go, Whit. His priority had to be getting his niece and brother back, so he pushed aside the sting of betrayal.

He opened the car's front door, shoved the airbag out of the way and checked Schneider's pulse.

He was okay; semiconscious. Whit grabbed the radio and called for help. He gave dispatch the plate number and description of the SUV. If they had any brains, they'd swap cars sooner rather than later.

Then again, if they had any brains they would not only have taken Whit's phone, but would have destroyed the patrol car's radio.

Well, that was good news. If they weren't all that bright they'd be easier to find.

Schneider moaned.

"You'll be okay," Whit said. "Help's on the way."

Would it arrive soon enough, or would Levi Moore flee the state with Whit's niece?

"I'm sorry, brother," Whit said. Oppressive guilt overwhelmed him. He was no hero. He did it again. He'd let his brother down.

Whit had trusted the wrong person, was falling in love with her and wasn't physically up to the challenge of protecting his niece.

And now he migt never see Harry or Mia again.

Back at the sheriff's office, Harper and his deputies formulated a game plan, while Whit struggled not to let his anger render him helpless.

"Why set up a meet?" Harper said.

"As a distraction," Whit said. "We were so intent on the meet-up that he caught us off guard."

"Carly took your phone?"

"Yes, to prevent me from calling for help."

"So she's been playing us? Man, I'd started to actually believe in her."

So had Whit. He'd believed in her, appreciated her and maybe even loved her.

"Harper," one of his deputies called from the other side of the room. The detective went to confer on something, leaving Whit to consider Harper's words.

Carly had been playing them, all of them. Especially Whit.

His gut burned with frustration. His blind trust in Carly had turned sour, eating away his insides.

Yet something felt off and he couldn't see the whole picture because his perception was blurred by betrayal.

God, help me see this a different way.

He closed his eyes and Carly's brilliant smile filled his mind, the sound of her singing to Mia, her voice infused with love. That was real. Her love for Mia was real.

This young woman, a gentle soul, had somehow managed to remain as Mia's nanny, even though it meant working for a crime family.

She'd also managed to prevent Levi's men from killing Whit.

Killing a cop will put a bull's-eye on our back and make it impossible to get out of town.

Amazing.

He could see it clearly now, see past his bruised ego and emotional pain. "Harper, can I use your computer?"

Harper joined him and logged in. "What've you got?"

"I think I know why she took my phone."

"To keep you from calling for help."

"I called it in on the radio. Taking my phone did nothing to prevent that."

"Then why'd she take it?"

"To help us find her."

Whit signed into his account and searched for his phone.

"Where's this?" Whit pointed to the screen.

"Small airport outside Denver. I'll notify the feds."

The SUV drove past a private airplane sitting outside a hangar and parked. Not good. Levi was no doubt planning to fly them away to parts unknown, never to be found again. Carly would be at the mercy of these criminals for who knows how long.

Find us, Whit, you have to find us.

As she exited the car, Levi was waiting for her, hands out, expecting to take Mia. Although Carly didn't want to relinquish the child, she had to keep playing the part of new employee for a notorious crime family.

She handed Mia to Levi and grabbed her purse and diaper bag. Mia squealed, disliking how this stranger awkwardly held her. Levi cringed at the sound of her cries.

"Here, let me." Carly took Mia. "I can teach you how she likes to be held, don't worry."

"Oh, I'm not worried." Levi shot her a creepy smile. "Follow me."

Girl, what have you gotten yourself into? She coached herself to stay strong as she considered strategy to stop from getting on that plane and vanishing forever.

Levi didn't escort her onto the plane. He led her to a small office, opened the door and there, on the floor with his hands bound behind him, head tipped down, sat Harry Bremerton.

"There's someone here to see you, Harry," Levi said.

Mr. Bremerton slowly looked up, bruises coloring his face. "Mia," he said, in a hoarse voice.

The little girl turned her head toward the sound of her father's voice and squealed with delight when she saw him. Mia reached out for her papa.

"Let me hold her," Mr. B. begged.

Carly automatically went toward him. Levi blocked her.

"You're not wearing a mask," Mr. B. said to his captor.

"I want you to remember my face." Levi

stepped closer. "The face of the man who took everything from you."

"Please...please let me hold her," Mr. B. pleaded.

"You've held her for the past seven months. Now it's my turn. And I'll get to hold her for the rest of her life."

"Mia," Mr. B. groaned.

"While you spend the rest of your life worrying about the little girl. Is she happy? Being well cared for? Has she joined the family business? You'll always wonder, and it will eat away at you like acid devouring metal."

Carly's heart was breaking for Mr. B.

His eyes reddened with tears. "Mia."

"That's no longer her name. From now on we'll call her—" Levi hesitated and glanced at Carly "—Greta."

A chill raced down Carly's spine. Oh, this guy had done his homework all right. He was not only messing with Mr. B.'s head, but Levi was playing mind games with Carly, as well.

Well, it was time for Carly to play some of her own games.

"I need to change the baby," she said, wrinkling her nose.

"The baby...?" Levi raised an eyebrow.

"Greta." She played along. "I need to change her diaper or she's going to stink up your plane."

Levi opened the office door and motioned to one of his men.

Carly tried sharing a sympathetic look with Mr. B. but he was staring at the floor, totally lost.

"Escort the nanny to the bathroom and wait while she changes my daughter's diaper, then get them on the plane," Levi said to his thug. "I'll be there shortly."

"Yes, sir."

Without looking at Levi, Carly stepped around him and followed the guy through the hangar. She didn't see the other two men. They must already be on the plane.

Mia still cried for her daddy and Carly soothed her, while scanning the area for a good hiding place to keep them safe until help arrived.

If Whit figured out her plan.

Fleeing the hangar wasn't an option. She and Mia wouldn't get far, and it would expose her ultimate goal: stop Levi from taking this child away from her adoptive parents.

The thug, who carried a gun in his hand as if expecting trouble, opened the bathroom door, and she peered inside. "I need something to lay the baby down on."

She noticed a horizontal storage container a few feet away. It was a big container, which gave her an idea. "This works."

She went to the locker, laid Mia down and placed a pacifier in her mouth to ease her anxiety.

The thug was antsy, probably worried about being caught by the cops. He took a few steps away and scanned the area. Carly worked up the courage to make her next move.

With one hand on the baby, she grabbed the weapon out of her purse. This was her best chance…

"Hey!"

The guy turned and she fired the Taser, nailing him in the chest. His body jerked and hit the ground.

There was no going back now. She picked up Mia and snatched the guy's gun off the floor. Opening the storage unit, she sighed with relief.

Praise God, it was empty.

She tossed the diaper bag around the corner, out of sight, and climbed into the storage unit holding Mia and the gun, although her finger was not on the trigger. Light shone through a crack in the lid. She adjusted the pacifier in Mia's mouth.

Please stay quiet, sweet thing.

"Where's my daughter?" Levi shouted. "Carter!"

"He's over here on the floor!" another guy said.

Carly's heart pounded up into her throat.

"Shh," she whispered to Mia. If the child made any sounds, even the slightest whimper…

"Find them!" Levi ordered. "Kill the nanny!"

He maketh me to lie down in green pastures: he leadeth me beside the still waters.

"We need to get on the plane!" one of the guys said.

"Not without my child!"

Mia suddenly squeaked.

Carly bit back a gasp.

"Over there!" Levi said.

They were close. Her heart pounded into her throat.

"Federal agents!"

Gunfire echoed throughout the hangar, making Mia burst into inconsolable sobs. Carly pinched her eyes shut, humming against the child's soft hair.

The shooting stopped suddenly. Mia's cries did not.

She clung to the baby, while holding the gun in her right hand. Could she use it to shoot and kill someone? Doubtful, although if she had to die it might as well be trying to save this little girl from a criminal monster.

Adrenaline blocked all sense of time. She could have been hiding there for minutes or hours, she wasn't sure.

The storage locker cracked open. She couldn't look, and she certainly wasn't letting go of Mia.

"I got 'em!" It was Whit's voice.

She gasped. Didn't realize she'd been holding her breath. She opened her eyes to the most beautiful sight: Whit's warm blue eyes and gentle expression.

"Nice hiding place," he said.

"Thanks."

"Ready to come out?"

"I think so."

She offered him the gun and he tucked it away, then helped her up. As she stood, he pulled her and Mia into a group hug. Peace flowed through her body. This man had come for her. He'd saved them both.

And she loved him with all her heart.

"The baby, is Mia okay?" Mr. B. said, rushing up to them.

Whit broke the embrace. Carly handed the baby to Mr. B.

"Susan?" he said, rocking Mia.

"She's okay, but traumatized."

"Serenity Resort was a fraud," Mr. B. said. "Susan had no idea. The kidnapping wasn't her fault."

"The kidnapping had nothing to do with Serenity Resort," Whit said. "The man who took you, Levi Moore, is Mia's biological father."

"I… I don't understand. The woman we adopted her from said she didn't know who the father was."

"She didn't want Levi coming after Mia," Carly said.

Mr. B. stared off into space, his face looking even paler.

Whit waved two EMTs over. "Let's get you to the hospital, Harry."

Mr. B. wouldn't let go of Mia.

"Come on, little brother. I got this," Whit said. He reached out and took Mia.

"You don't know anything about kids," Mr. B. said, climbing onto a stretcher.

"Yeah, funny thing, I got a crash course this week." He glanced at Carly. "Had a great teacher."

Mr. B. reached out and squeezed Carly's hand. "Thank you."

"Of course."

The EMTs wheeled him away.

"We'll be right behind you," Whit called.

Carly and Whit headed out of the hangar toward Detective Harper's car.

"What about Levi?" she said.

"He was shot and killed by federal agents. Two of his men were critically injured, and the third, well, someone shot him with a Taser." He quirked an eyebrow.

"I'm a pretty good shot."

"Maybe with a Taser, but the gun you handed me? The safety was on."

"Not sure I could have used it anyway."

They walked in silence for a few seconds. Now that the case was resolved, and life would go back to normal, an unexpected awkwardness grew between them.

"Thanks for finding us," she said.

"I was confused at first, when you took my phone—"

"You thought I was joining the other side, huh?"

Whit shrugged. "Not for long."

"I knew you'd figure it out." She smiled.

* * *

The woman's smile lit up Whit's heart. He'd never experienced this kind of connection and it wasn't because they'd met during a high-adrenaline situation. He knew in his heart that no matter how they met they'd develop a connection beyond ordinary friendship or romantic love.

"Carly, once everything settles down—"

"I know, you'll be going back to your job in Dallas, and I'll take the nurse's exam. Everything will get back to normal."

Whit didn't want *normal*. He wanted Carly.

"Actually, I was thinking I might hang around Miner for a while, reconnect with my brother, spend some time with my niece, maybe even ask her nanny out for dinner."

"And then you'll return Texas," she said.

He hesitated, realizing he had no real desire to return to the department. After everything that happened this week, he felt like his hero complex, the need to catch the bad guys and protect the world, was interfering with something more important: his desire to reconnect with his brother, with family, which had been missing from his life.

He couldn't do that from eight hundred miles away.

Frustration had consumed him when he'd been benched because of his injuries on the job. Somehow that frustration had dissolved and today everything looked different, it felt different, and he wondered if maybe God had something else planned for him.

God? Since when have you considered God's plans?

Since Carly entered his life.

Mia lunged sideways, reaching for Carly. Whit handed her over and said, "I like the weather better in Denver."

"It's definitely gorgeous in the summer."

"As opposed to a hundred-plus degrees in Texas."

There was a long, awkward pause. "I can't believe we're talking about the weather," Whit said.

Carly smiled. And he was lost yet again. Or make that…found.

He was about to officially ask her on a date when Harper interrupted them. "The feds need Carly's statement."

"Oh, okay." Carly handed the baby back to Whit.

As she walked away with one of the federal agents, she glanced over her shoulder and shared a half smile with Whit.

"I'll see you later," he called out.

Whit turned to get into Harper's car and the detective cracked a half smile, shaking his head. "You are in trouble, my friend."

During the next few weeks, everyone struggled to get back to normal: Susan and Harry, the doting parents, Susan now a cooperating witness for the prosecution into the fraud scheme; Whit playing his part of overprotective brother and uncle; and Carly, the loving nanny.

Even though something had significantly changed between him and Carly, Whit still felt a connection. He assumed she was stressed about her upcoming nurse's exam and therefore he decided to give her space.

That didn't stop him from sharing a smile now and then.

Whit and Harry were talking and drinking coffee one night when Carly entered the kitchen.

"She needs her nighttime bottle," Carly explained and proceeded to open the refrigerator.

"Susan will be okay," Harry said. "At least legally."

"And emotionally?" Whit asked.

"She's still struggling with the trauma."

"Who wouldn't be after everything she's endured," Carly chimed in, and then glanced at the men. "Sorry, didn't mean to insert myself into your conversation."

"No apologies necessary," Harry said. "You're more like a part of the family than an employee."

"Thanks. I've been wondering how Sam's doing."

"She's physically on the mend," Whit said. "Decided to cooperate with the feds, filling in the blanks about Levi's business, which means she may need to go into witness protection."

"So she won't be able to see Mia," Carly said softly.

"Sam still wants Harry and Susan to raise Mia. Nothing's changed there," Whit said.

Carly nodded. "Well, I'd better get the bottle up to the little one. Mrs. B. wants to feed her while I read a bedtime story."

"Tell Susan I'll be up in a few minutes," Harry said.

"Will do." She glanced at Whit and a slight smile curved her lips. She turned and left.

"Really?" Harry said.

Whit snapped his attention to his brother. "What?"

"We were kidnapped and you were making a play for the nanny?"

"It wasn't like that."

"Yeah, okay," Harry teased.

Whit smiled and stirred his coffee. "Can I ask you something?"

"Of course."

"What happened last month? I mean, I thought we were reconnecting and then you stopped returning my calls."

"I started to suspect something was off with Serenity Resort. I was embarrassed, ashamed, didn't want you to know."

"You didn't do anything wrong."

"On some level I felt responsible."

"Come again?"

"Perhaps if I'd been more attentive to my wife, Susan wouldn't have thrown herself into all these projects. She might have paid more attention and not been manipulated by the Serenity scheme. It was so important that I be proud of her. I told her what a great mom she was, but I guess she didn't think that was enough."

"And Mia, why didn't you tell me she was adopted?"

"I planned to, eventually, but you and I were just starting to reconnect. Susan was terribly insecure about our inability to conceive and wanted to keep it private. The adoption wasn't something we broadcast, although a few close friends from church knew. The thought of losing Mia…" He sighed and stared into his coffee. "One thing's for sure, I'm going to spend more time with my family and less time at the office."

"Sounds like a good plan to me."

"My turn to ask you something," Harry said. "You don't seem to be in a hurry to return to Texas."

"They haven't cleared me to go back to work."

"And when they do?"

Whit shrugged. "I guess I'm starting to think other things might be more important than the job."

"Mia got to you, didn't she? Or was it the nanny?"

Whit shrugged. "A little of both?"

"Good, because this experience has inspired a new business venture and I think you're the perfect guy to help me get it started."

"Yeah? What's that?"

"Private security."

"For...?"

"For my family, for starters, then we can branch out."

"Ah, you're feeling sorry for me."

"Hardly. You protected my daughter. You're great at what you do."

"Carly deserves some credit. If she hadn't left the house with Mia the day you were taken..." Whit's voice trailed off and he shook his head.

"She's a special woman and we're blessed to have her in our lives. I'm also feeling very blessed, sitting here, drinking coffee with my big brother. There was a time when I didn't think that would ever happen."

"I know, and I'm sorry."

"You're sorry?"

"For being the negligent brother. You got hurt on my watch. I figured that's why you kept your distance from me, from the family. Why you were so angry with us."

"I was angry because you abandoned me."

"I felt guilty that I'd failed you."

"Brody, you were seventeen and I was a dumb kid trying to impress his big brother. I got hurt, and you left. Therefore, it was my fault that you abandoned us. After you did great things in the army and joined the police force, Mom constantly talked about what a hero you were. I couldn't live up to your reputation, and I grew resentful because you were out there taking care of other people, but you didn't have time for your little brother. It was eating away at me. Susan convinced me to pray, to ask God for guidance. Through my faith, I learned that resentment destroys us, whereas forgiveness is the path to grace. I forgave you and had to forgive myself for holding a grudge. A few months later I was still trying to figure out how to reach out to you when you called."

"Man, I'm glad I did."

"Me, too. Can you forgive me for being such a blockhead?"

"That's a silly question," Whit said. When he glanced up at his brother, Harry looked like a kid again, desperately needing his brother's approval, and love. "Of course I forgive you, Harry."

Harry visibly exhaled. "Good, good." He placed his hand on Whit's shoulder. "Consider my offer about private security?"

Whit nodded that he would.

"Well, I'd better go up and kiss my daughter good-night."

When Harry stood, he paused, and the men embraced, something they hadn't done in years. Tears burned Whit's eyes. Tears of joy.

* * *

Carly came out of the testing facility and breathed in the fresh Colorado air. She was proud of herself for managing to do her best work given the trauma she was still processing from the kidnapping case.

As she headed down the sidewalk, she noticed a familiar figure sitting on a bench up ahead.

Whit.

Holding a bouquet of flowers. How curious. He'd distanced himself from her in the past few weeks, and every morning she fully expected to wake up and hear he'd gone back to Dallas. She assumed that he'd decided their intimacy was born of the high-adrenaline time they spent together protecting Mia.

That it wasn't real.

"Hi, Whit. What are you doing here?" she said.

"How'd it go?"

"I think okay."

He stood and handed her the bouquet. "Congratulations on finishing the exam."

"Wow, thanks. They're beautiful. I've gotta say, I'm kind of surprised."

"You don't think I'm a classy enough guy to give a girl flowers?"

"No, I thought you'd lost interest. We haven't spoken much since, you know."

"I didn't want to distract you from your studies."

"You should've said so." She playfully slugged

him in the arm, then quickly withdrew her fist. "Sorry, sorry. Just what you don't need is me making your injury worse to prevent you from returning to work."

"You didn't hit me that hard," he said lightly. "Besides, I've been offered a new job, here in Colorado."

"What kind of job?"

"My brother wants me to start a security branch of his company, so we'll be working closely together. Let's hope we don't strangle each other," he teased. "You be sure to spray us with the hose if you find us fighting in the yard."

"Will do." She could hardly contain her excitement. He was staying in Miner?

He handed her a white envelope.

"What's this?" she said.

"Your sister's contact information."

Carly froze and looked at him. "I didn't ask you to do that."

"I know. I hope you're not angry. I figured, well, if I was able to mend things with my brother, you could, too. When you're ready."

She studied the envelope in her hand. "Now I have to do something."

"No, you don't. But you don't have to be tormented either. She's done well for herself, Carly. She's okay."

Carly nodded. "I'm glad." She slipped the envelope into her purse and they walked side by side. Knowing Greta was okay almost made Carly burst into tears of relief and gratitude.

"Uh-oh. I blew it, didn't I?" Whit said.

"What?"

"You and me, keeping my distance so you could concentrate on the test?"

"No." She smiled. "I get it now."

"Great. So, how about that dinner?"

"I have to get back to the house."

"Actually, you don't. I negotiated a night off. I thought we could celebrate."

"What, me taking the test?"

"Nah, I thought we could celebrate this." He leaned forward and kissed her.

It felt completely natural, like they'd kissed before, many times. Gentle and warm and perfect.

He broke the kiss and continued walking. "Do you have a preference?"

Sure, she had a preference. She wanted him to kiss her again.

"Of restaurants?" he prompted.

"It doesn't matter as long as I'm with you, Brody Whittaker. As long as I'm with you."

And this time, it was her turn to kiss him.

* * * * *

Dear Reader,

In my experience I've learned that it's never too late to forgive someone—or ourselves for that matter—even if we're not sure they are worthy of it. After all, if God forgives, then who are we not to forgive, especially when it ultimately leads to emotional peace?

Our mistakes in life are just that, mistakes. Those misjudgments create our life experience and make us who we are. Mistakes can teach us valuable lessons and show us how to be humble, a very important trait.

Carly and Brody suffer from deep emotional wounds born of guilt. They each shoulder a lot of regret over decisions they made years ago. Throughout the course of the book, they are challenged to put aside their guilt and open their hearts to forgiveness. These two wounded souls are able to help each other grow and embrace the serenity that is on the other side of forgiveness.

My goal in writing this story was to share with you my belief that it's never too late to forgive, and to illustrate how the power of forgiveness can heal emotional pain and guide us to the beauty of grace.

Peace be with you,
Hope White

Get 4 FREE REWARDS!

We'll send you 2 FREE Books plus 2 FREE Mystery Gifts.

Love Inspired® books feature contemporary inspirational romances with Christian characters facing the challenges of life and love.

FREE Value Over $20

YES! Please send me 2 FREE Love Inspired® Romance novels and my 2 FREE mystery gifts (gifts are worth about $10 retail). After receiving them, if I don't wish to receive any more books, I can return the shipping statement marked "cancel." If I don't cancel, I will receive 6 brand-new novels every month and be billed just $5.24 for the regular-print edition or $5.74 each for the larger-print edition in the U.S., or $5.74 each for the regular-print edition or $6.24 each for the larger-print edition in Canada. That's a savings of at least 13% off the cover price. It's quite a bargain! Shipping and handling is just 50¢ per book in the U.S. and 75¢ per book in Canada.* I understand that accepting the 2 free books and gifts places me under no obligation to buy anything. I can always return a shipment and cancel at any time. The free books and gifts are mine to keep no matter what I decide.

Choose one: ☐ **Love Inspired® Romance Regular-Print** (105/305 IDN GMY4) ☐ **Love Inspired® Romance Larger-Print** (122/322 IDN GMY4)

Name (please print)

Address   Apt. #

City   State/Province   Zip/Postal Code

Mail to the Reader Service:
IN U.S.A.: P.O. Box 1341, Buffalo, NY 14240-8531
IN CANADA: P.O. Box 603, Fort Erie, Ontario L2A 5X3

Want to try 2 free books from another series? Call 1-800-873-8635 or visit www.ReaderService.com.

---

*Terms and prices subject to change without notice. Prices do not include sales taxes, which will be charged (if applicable) based on your state or country of residence. Canadian residents will be charged applicable taxes. Offer not valid in Quebec. This offer is limited to one order per household. Books received may not be as shown. Not valid for current subscribers to Love Inspired Romance books. All orders subject to approval. Credit or debit balances in a customer's account(s) may be offset by any other outstanding balance owed by or to the customer. Please allow 4 to 6 weeks for delivery. Offer available while quantities last.

Your Privacy—The Reader Service is committed to protecting your privacy. Our Privacy Policy is available online at www.ReaderService.com or upon request from the Reader Service. We make a portion of our mailing list available to reputable third parties that offer products we believe may interest you. If you prefer that we not exchange your name with third parties, or if you wish to clarify or modify your communication preferences, please visit us at www.ReaderService.com/consumerschoice or write to us at Reader Service Preference Service, P.O. Box 9062, Buffalo, NY 14240-9062. Include your complete name and address.

LI19R2

Get 4 FREE REWARDS!

We'll send you 2 FREE Books plus 2 FREE Mystery Gifts.

Harlequin® Heartwarming™ Larger-Print books feature traditional values of home, family, community and—most of all—love.

FREE Value Over $20

YES! Please send me 2 FREE Harlequin® Heartwarming™ Larger-Print novels and my 2 FREE mystery gifts (gifts worth about $10 retail). After receiving them, if I don't wish to receive any more books, I can return the shipping statement marked "cancel." If I don't cancel, I will receive 4 brand-new larger-print novels every month and be billed just $5.49 per book in the U.S. or $6.24 per book in Canada. That's a savings of at least 19% off the cover price. It's quite a bargain! Shipping and handling is just 50¢ per book in the U.S. and 75¢ per book in Canada.* I understand that accepting the 2 free books and gifts places me under no obligation to buy anything. I can always return a shipment and cancel at any time. The free books and gifts are mine to keep no matter what I decide.

161/361 IDN GMY3

Name (please print)

Address   Apt. #

City   State/Province   Zip/Postal Code

Mail to the **Reader Service:**
IN U.S.A.: P.O. Box 1341, Buffalo, NY 14240-8531
IN CANADA: P.O. Box 603, Fort Erie, Ontario L2A 5X3

Want to try 2 free books from another series? Call 1-800-873-8635 or visit www.ReaderService.com.

*Terms and prices subject to change without notice. Prices do not include sales taxes, which will be charged (if applicable) based on your state or country of residence. Canadian residents will be charged applicable taxes. Offer not valid in Quebec. This offer is limited to one order per household. Books received may not be as shown. Not valid for current subscribers to Harlequin Heartwarming Larger-Print books. All orders subject to approval. Credit or debit balances in a customer's account(s) may be offset by any other outstanding balance owed by or to the customer. Please allow 4 to 6 weeks for delivery. Offer available while quantities last.

Your Privacy—The Reader Service is committed to protecting your privacy. Our Privacy Policy is available online at www.ReaderService.com or upon request from the Reader Service. We make a portion of our mailing list available to reputable third parties that offer products we believe may interest you. If you prefer that we not exchange your name with third parties, or if you wish to clarify or modify your communication preferences, please visit us at www.ReaderService.com/consumerschoice or write to us at Reader Service Preference Service, P.O. Box 9062, Buffalo, NY 14240-9062. Include your complete name and address.

HW19R2

COMING NEXT MONTH FROM
Love Inspired® Suspense

Available August 6, 2019

SEEKING THE TRUTH
True Blue K-9 Unit • by Terri Reed
By investigating the murder of the NYPD K-9 Command Unit chief, reporter Rachelle Clark draws a killer's attention. And if she wants to stay alive, relying on the late chief's handsome brother, Officer Carter Jameson, and his K-9 partner is suddenly her only option.

THE CRADLE CONSPIRACY
The Baby Protectors • by Christy Barritt
With someone willing to kill to get to the little boy Sienna Thompson's babysitting, her next-door neighbor, FBI agent Devin Matthews, vows to protect her and the two-year-old. But when they discover the child's mother isn't who she claimed to be, can they survive long enough to uncover the truth?

MARKED FOR REVENGE
Emergency Responders • by Valerie Hansen
When EMT Kaitlin North realizes a gunshot-wound patient is the police officer who once saved her life, she's determined to return the favor. But with a price on Daniel Ryan's head and no one to trust, can she hide him from the hit men?

LOST RODEO MEMORIES
by Jenna Night
After Melanie Graham awakens in the woods with a head injury and no memory of what happened, she quickly learns that someone wants her dead. Can sheriff's deputy Luke Baxter keep her safe as he works to identify the unknown assailant?

SECURITY MEASURES
by Sara K. Parker
To halt a killing spree, bodyguard Triss Everett tightens security at the senior community where she volunteers—and makes herself a target. Her coworker, widowed single father Hunter Knox, won't let her become the next victim. But as Hunter fights for Triss's life, he finds himself also fighting for her love.

INTENSIVE CARE CRISIS
by Karen Kirst
Reporting missing medical supplies and narcotics lands nurse Audrey Harris and her patients right in the crosshairs of a ruthless thief. But when Force Recon marine sergeant Julian is one of the patients in danger, the criminals unwittingly provide her with a strong—and handsome—protector.

LOOK FOR THESE AND OTHER LOVE INSPIRED BOOKS WHEREVER BOOKS ARE SOLD, INCLUDING MOST BOOKSTORES, SUPERMARKETS, DISCOUNT STORES AND DRUGSTORES.

LISLPCNMBPA0719